ABOUT THE AUTHOR

Werner J. Egli is an accomplished Swiss writer with novels for all ages, published in German-speaking Europe, where he received some of the most prestigious awards for his writing. His books are translated into many other languages. He got nominated for the Hans Christian Andersen-medal after Tunnel Kids was published. It is his first novel translated into English. Werner J. Egli lives near Zurich, Switzerland and in Tucson, Arizona.

WERNER J. EGLI

TUNNEL KIDS

A NOVEL

Published by ARAVAIPA-Verlag
Zelgmatt 24, CH-8132 EGG bei Zürich, Switzerland
First published in Germany by C. Bertelsmann/Random House, Munich,1999
Copyright by Werner J. Egli, 2017
All rights reserved
ISBN: 978-3-03864-408-8
Jacket design: flin
Jacket art: Bert Silberstein
Translation: James Pierce
Edited by Esther Porter

Acknowlegments

I would like to thank Melissa Gray, who worked as a first draft proofreader on this book, to Marlies Single and to James Pierce, who helped me get it started.

For my kids, Tamara, Dunja, Lara and Nicolas and for my grandson Yannick.

SAN CRISTÓBAL DE LAS CASAS, Mexico

"Indian rebels retreated into the jungle yesterday, leaving three villages to the 12,000 soldiers who have entered this remote region of Mexico to put down a bloody rebellion."

The Arizona Daily Star, January 1994

"They call them tunnel rats. It is easier for a society that labels its children as vermin to treat them as vermin."

The Arizona Daily Star, May 1994

***

1
Santiago

The photo was of my mother, but it was also the memory of the day a tourist bus strayed into our village. Santa Claus staggered out of the American bar on his way to the soccer field where all the children were supposed to get a present.

Santa Claus was a gringo. The people of our village called him Papa Biddle. Once, he bribed me with a dollar not to tell my father about how I'd surprised him grabbing my sister under her skirt with his fleshy gringo hand as he was telling her a funny story.

I would often think back to that Christmas day. Because of all the festivities, it did not fit into the life I was accustomed to. Shortly before noon, Papa Biddle stepped out of the American bar and went across the street, listing to one side, and through the soccer field to behind the goal in the forest's shade. We had all gathered there, about two hundred children from the entire region, some from even farther away, from around Rio Pequi and from the village of San Isidro. We each got our present from the Red Cross by way of Papa Biddle's trembling gringo hand, his fingernails as brown from smoking fat cigars as his few remaining teeth.

My mother, my sister Theresa, and my brothers Miguelito and Francisco were there. Mother had the baby, Paolita, in her arms. And, suddenly, this small tourist bus halted at the edge of the soccer field, which was also the marketplace and fiesta-place for our little village. And then people from all over the world that had come here to see us, the descendants of the Maya Empire, moved hurriedly across the rough plaza, where the grass grew so sparsely that not a single goat could grow fat on it.

One of the tourists, a gringo with a goatee and a wallet that hung heavily in the back pocket of his baggy pants, took

7

a flash photograph of my mother just as Papa Biddle leaned forward with his flowing beard to give Paolita her Christmas present. The baby screamed, and Mother looked distraught, probably because Biddle had just exhaled his whiskey breath directly in her face. The gringo with the goatee had pressed the camera button at the same time, the flash startling her. This photo was my strongest memory from that day. The gringo took it with a Polaroid camera, and seconds later he proudly showed it around before he handed it over to my mother. It was a wonder in a day full of wonders, which were happening only in my head, as I sent my most secret wishes to Heaven, along with the cloud rising from the men of our village. They all sat in front of a bodega, completely bored, smoking, drinking beer and watching Papa Biddle parcel out the presents. They also looked at my mother, who had once been the most beautiful of all the women in our village, more desirable even than my sister Theresa.

That Christmas now lay four years back. My mother's face at the stench of Biddle's whiskey-filled breath, the terror in the baby's wide-open eyes and Papa Biddle's furrowed, bulbous nose, red as a rotting strawberry.

It was not the photo itself that I had carried with me since then; instead, it was my memory of it. I did not know who had that picture now, or whether it still existed. For a while, Mother had it hanging in our hut. Then, when Father left our village, Los Chorros, to join Subcomandante Marcos in the revolution for justice, freedom, and democracy, it disappeared. I think, at the time, Father had it in the breast pocket of his old jacket, directly over his heart. Later, when he returned, and everyone thought the revolution was over and that the government would at least return a bit of our land to us, it was again in our home. When I looked at it closely the last time, there were dark spots on it, and I knew that they were flecks of my father's blood. Maybe it is still hanging there, fastened with a nail to one of the posts that held up the roof.

Biddle died in the meantime. He drank himself to death in the American bar. Theresa had been working for several months as a waitress in there. She no longer lived with us, but with a young man named Hector, who worked at a sawmill where they cut trees into lumber. They lived in a hut near Acteal, provided by the company that ran the sawmill. Theresa never stayed at our home anymore. She came only once to get her things from under her bed. I asked her if she was going to marry Hector. She laughed and said that she had no intention of marrying anybody. But she was pregnant. I heard her fighting with Mother, who called her a person with no sense of responsibility, just like the whores in the bars of big towns. Theresa ran out of the house to where Hector was waiting for her in a pickup truck that belonged to the company. Before she climbed in, she looked around once more not wanting her heart to forget where she had come from—her bundle pressed to her as if it were a baby.

A few weeks after Theresa left, they took Paolita and Francisco away. Mother had given them up for adoption because our life could no longer be called life; instead, it was torture. At the time, I did not understand adoption. It was only a word to me, nothing else. Only when some people from the city came and took Paolita and Francisco—only then did I understand what was happening. I could see it in my mother's dark eyes. I could see the pain in them, the sorrow. I ran into the forest and cried my soul out of my body. I knew that, because of my father's murder, our family had ceased to exist. It was destroyed, our blood-bond torn apart. When I came home, Mother was in the field. Miguelito sat in the hut and stared into a hole. Mother had not given him up for adoption. Nobody would have wanted him. From his birth, something was not right in his head. So nobody wanted to have him, except for my mother. She loved him more than Paolita or Francisco, perhaps even more than me.

I thought about it for a long time, but I never understood why Mother did not give me away too. I thought about it every day for weeks, especially at night when I couldn't sleep. Maybe I was too old. Too rebellious. Too convinced I would go my way, undeterred by anyone or anything.

"Your son is dangerous," the men who thought they knew me had warned her.

"You give this boy his way, and there will be a disaster," they said. "He cannot be satisfied with his lot in life."

And so it was. I thought I might kill someone if they put me up for adoption. I was ready. Death did not scare me anymore. Death was my friend—a liberator from pain. Whoever gave their lives to it found peace.

My mother and I hardly spoke to each other anymore.

Then, when the long rains were over, I took the wallet I had pulled from the gringo's baggy pants pocket four years back, and I left our village.

I went northward along the old cart road through the forest. For the first two days, I hid in the undergrowth whenever I encountered someone. On the third day, I came to the city of Tuxtla Gutiérrez. I went to a store and bought a pair of proper shoes, a pair of pants and a shirt. I also purchased a hat because the shady forest stopped here at the bank of the river, and beyond lay open land where the sun burned down. I left the city in the night and walked in the moonlight through the open country until I was tired. Then I lay down and slept with the wallet in my pocket and my right hand tightly gripped around the machete I had brought with me from home.

It was this way every day and every night. I was a stranger in a strange world, a descendant of the Maya empire. My mother tongue was not that of the people with whom I came into contact. I learned Spanish in our village school, but my native language was Tzotzil. To everyone who was not one of us, I was a Tzotzil Indian.

I did not trust anyone and nobody trusted me on my way north to the big city. The capital. Twenty million people lived there. I tried to imagine how it looked from high above. Like a colony of millions of ants on a hill, I guessed. And I was one of them, the only one who didn't know anything about anything, just roamed around aimlessly, sometimes here, sometimes there. Crossing the streets on the red light. "Hey, are you colorblind, kid?" Against the flow of hurrying people. "Get away, kid." And stepping on all kinds of people's feet. "Excuse me," I'd say, to which the response usually was something like "Pay more attention to where you're walking, you filthy little bastard."

It seemed I was nothing but a wretch without a home or family. Outwardly, I was no different than the other ants. But I did not belong. I was an outsider. A dangerous little scoundrel no one had better get in the way of.

A kid stood next to a stand where there was cold soda. He was a boy scarcely older than I was. He stood there staring at me with a smile.

"Where are you from, my friend?" he asked, perhaps feeling like nothing more than an ant himself, young like me and maybe without a home or family, although he did not look as run down.

"Chiapas," I said and paid for the glass of soda.

"Chiapas is far away," he said.

"Very."

"Do you have a name?"

"Santiago Molina."

"Jesus." He stretched out his hand, which was missing two fingers. "Like He who got nailed to the cross for your sins."

"What about your sins?" I answered.

"You can trust me," he laughed. "I am like you."

I looked him in the eyes. He was not like me. He was like Jesus. Soft and without deceit. His eyes were like my mother's, and hers had been like Maria's, the holy one, until Father's blood had covered the picture in my head. My mother's name was Maria and, to me, in my early youth, she was like her too.

"I'll bet that you want to go to America," said Jesus.

He meant the United States of America. I had learned that in school. That everything was America here. From Tierra del Fuego to Alaska. America. It was my land; Indian land was stolen from us, for which my father had fought at the side of Subcomandante Marcos. But when people like me traveled, they traveled to foreign parts. To America. The United States. The land of the proud and free. The land of gringos Papa Biddle called it, even though he was one himself.

"I don't know where I'm going," I said.

"Bet you're going to America."

We shook hands, and he said that he knew where I could spend the night.

"My mother will make you a meal, and you can sleep in my bed," he said. "You evidently haven't slept in a regular bed for many days."

"Weeks," I said.

*

I went with him, diagonally through the city, through crowds of people in the streets. He cleared a path for me, using his elbows to do so. No, he was not Jesus. People did not step back from him, nor bow to him respectfully. He did not lay hands on the heads of any of the crippled beggars hunkered before the old churches and on the marble benches to free them from their pains and cares. He pushed people out of the way. He bumped into a man who came out of a store. He ran across the street between honking automobiles, leading the way for me. He laughed as one of the drivers shouted angrily at him and shook his fist and pounded a dented fender. He spat against a dirt-smeared windshield, the car horns calling to us as if they were a pack of chained animals.

"This city is Hell," he said. "A person breathes in more exhaust than air. The water makes you sick, and if you find a place to lie down and die, the rats eat the sandals off your feet before you're even dead."

"Why don't you live somewhere else?"

"Where else would I want to live?"

I ran along with him blindly until we came to a sheet-metal hut, where his friends waited for him. There were four of them, including a girl wearing torn jeans and a T-shirt full of holes.

"This is Santiago," he said to them. "He is on his way to America." They studied me. It was as if he had told them that I had come from another planet, a little green man from space. Only the girl smiled at me. For some reason, that scared me.

*

"Where have you hidden your money?" one of them asked me.

"I don't have any money," I lied.

"You don't want to have any money?"

"I don't have any money."

He walked around me and stopped behind my back. I sensed him behind me, but I did not turn toward him. I did not risk looking at the girl. I looked at Jesus. I looked into his eyes.

"I told you," he said. "This city is Hell, and a name like mine is only a camouflage."

The one standing behind me blew cigarette smoke onto the back of my neck.

"I'll ask you once more," he said. "Where have you hidden your money?"

"Tell him before he gets angry," the girl demanded. Better tell him where you've hidden the money."

"If I had any money, I would give it to you."

"Then take off your pants."

"No, I won't do that."

"You should undress," said the girl.

"Do what he says," said Jesus.

"I'm going now," I said while I moved toward the door. I wanted to get out of this tin shack, where the floor was as black as tightly packed coal and stank of motor oil. To get out the door I moved toward the strips of light shining between the metal pieces, but the girl and the two others blocked my way.

"You can all see what is in my bag," I said. The bag lay on the floor. They searched through it and scattered my stuff across the floor. They didn't want it. Only the machete got their interest. One of them picked it up from the floor and held it in his hand. He grinned at me showing me my machete.

The one standing behind me pushed the glowing tip of his cigarette into my neck. The sudden pain made me cry out because I was not expecting it. Pain like I had never experienced before.

*

He stood over me with his legs spread apart and he looked big and vicious. I only saw him vaguely in the low light.

He smoked a cigarette, and the ash fell through a strip of sunlight, breaking into small flecks that fluttered down to me. He raised a foot and stepped on my midsection.

"You're lucky," he said. "You're lucky we don't kill you."

I wanted to tell him that he should kill me, but I couldn't put the words together. Something wasn't working right in my mind. My thoughts filled with all sorts of possibilities all jumbled together. Why don't you go ahead and kill me, you bastard. It raged inside my brain, but it never left my lips. I thought about the photo. My mother's face. Papa Biddle's rotten strawberry of a nose. Paolita's eyes.

My eyes saw something else. My eyes looked back to Los Chorros and into our hut, where my brother Miguelito stared at a hole that he had dug in the floor with a stick. He simply stared into the hole, where a small bug had fallen in and was trying to climb out unsuccessfully.

Blood smells good, my head thought. Better than motor oil.

I was freezing because I was naked.

The girl looked at me. She didn't smile anymore. She was afraid. Now, it was the girl who was afraid. Not me. I was at home. I saw the bug crawl out of the hole, and I saw Miguelito jump up and step on it.

Jesus stood at the door.

"Okay?" one of the others asked him.

Jesus opened the door a crack. Glaring sunlight transformed him into a shadow. He stuck his head through the gap.

"Okay," he said.

The others went out. Only Jesus remained. He looked at me.

"I'm sorry that I had to disappoint you," he said. "We could be brothers and it would not be any different. In our world, you can't trust anybody."

Now, he left too. He left me behind in the hut, and I lay there and closed my burning eyes. My heart pounded as if it wanted to explode. I had blood in my mouth and my nose. They had beaten me with their fists and with a piece of a water pipe until I fell to my knees. They hit me in the head with a brick, and they burned me with the glowing ends of their cigarettes as I lay naked on the floor.

I wanted to die, but I could not. Then, I wanted to live. I pulled together all my strength and pulled on my pants and shirt. They had taken my shoes with them. I picked up my bag from the floor and put my stuff they'd left behind back in. It was dark when I left the hut.

The city rumbled in the night that was not night. Lights everywhere. A sea of lights. Light and noise. The sky was light, but there were no stars. No moon. Light, bright and streaming and dirty like the humid night air.

I went down a street and in the dim light of a lamp, at a fountain dedicated to an angel, a man lay there on the ground, an old man on whose furrowed face the lamplight shone mercilessly. The white stubble of his beard glittered. His mouth was half opened, but he did not breathe. The man was dead. He had come here to drink some water. The stone angel looked down at him with one eye. Someone had knocked the other eye out. I drank the water, which did not taste like water. I washed the blood from my face, cleaning my wounds. I cooled the aching burns in my skin.

In a park, I lay down, hiding deep in the shadow of leafy bushes. I thought about the rats. I fell asleep and woke up with a dog licking my face.

2
Captain Mendoza

The small dog was a shaggy cur that smelled like garbage. It had a red leather band around its neck and a piece missing from its floppy left ear. I liked dogs. At home, there was always one roaming around thinking it belonged to us. My brother Francisco was bitten once by a bitch. Javier Chavez, the police officer at Los Chorros, had shot and killed her after that. Because dogs, he said, had no right to bite people.

This dog with one and a half ears probably thought I needed a friend. As I woke up and pushed him away, he began to bark at me.

"What do you want?" I asked him.

He raced around me in a circle, jumping over my outstretched legs. His floppy ear fluttered next to his head, and the other was half raised. He raced around me, barking as if possessed by the Devil. I tried to catch him, but he easily evaded my hand.

"Stop it," I shouted at him. "I'm getting dizzy."

He stopped and lay down in the grass a few feet away, panting. His eyes were half closed, and he acted as if he were looking past me. He was waiting for me to try to grab him. If I moved only a single finger, he stopped panting. He wanted to show me how intelligent and quick he was and that it would be impossible for me to get a hold of him.

"You're not as sly as you think," I said.

He grinned at me, his tongue hanging out the side of his mouth.

"It's just that I don't think I can take on a dog. I wouldn't know what to feed you."

I was hungry myself. The last things I had eaten were a couple of refried bean tacos.

"Come here."

The dog just lay there.

"You better come here."

He did not obey. I found a few dried tortilla crumbs in my pocket. I put them in my hand and offered them to him. He did not move off his spot. I licked the crumbs out of my hand and lay back down. I had no idea what time it was. Middle of the night it seemed. Maybe three o'clock. I lay there and could not go back to sleep. My body ached. It took me a while to get used to the pain. I got up and went to the park. The dog followed me. I picked up a stone and threw it at him. I didn't mean to hit him, only to make him go away, but I hit him on the leg. He jumped back and snapped at the leg as if a wasp had stung him there.

"See, you'd be better off if you'd get lost."

I went on. He followed me through the night, sometimes merely a shadow. He followed me through early morning. Then he disappeared. When I turned to look for him, I saw him in the shadow of a giant building—a museum. He was limping. I began to run, but I stopped again soon, because my entire body hurt. It hurt so much that I had to clench my teeth. I sat on the steps of an old church in the warm morning sun. Below, on the plaza, someone pushed a handcart to the edge of the street. He unfolded a box, and three or four metal buckets came to light. The box lid became a shelf where he lined up bottles that each contained liquid of a different color. Some were green. Some were red, yellow and blue. Like the vivid colors of a rainbow. He stretched open a sunshade and hung a sign on the stand: Cold soda for every taste.

Two old ladies came up the steps and disappeared into the church. A nun bought soda for a small child. Raspberry. The child and the nun went on, hand in hand, sharing the soda between themselves. I greeted the nun when she looked up at me. She nodded to me as if she knew something about me nobody else knew. I searched my conscience. There was nothing. Not even a trace, nada.

I stood and then I limped up the granite steps to the door. It was so cold in the church that I began to shiver. I sat down on a bench in the back, next to a niche where a saint made of stone stood on bare feet, a crucifix in his hands. The way he looked at me made me feel uneasy. On the pedestal before his bare feet lay a small offering plate with a few coins in it. This offering plate was not a plate at all; it was a basket with a small opening in its leather top. The opening was held small by a cord that could be opened to enlarge the hole and take the collected money out of the basket. I remember thinking, heck, they don't seem to trust some people not to get tempted and steal from the basket even though the saint held a rather watchful eye on that money. About three or four dozen candles were burning, but only a few coins lay in the basket, twinkling in the candlelight. My thoughts began to race. I thought about my father who was in Heaven, if there was a Heaven. It was also possible that he was in Hell, because he had a history of smashing my mother's teeth when he'd come home drunk. "Wherever you are, may it go well with you," I prayed. I stood up. As I left, I quickly opened the string and reached into the basket to sort out a few coins. I put them in my pocket and immediately left the church, running down the steps despite the aches and pains. The dog waited below. He looked at me the way the nun had earlier. As if he knew I had stolen from God. I got angry and kicked him in the stomach. It came as a surprise to him, and he yelped and jumped back. Then he followed me at a distance.

I went across the plaza into a narrow side street, where night shadows still nestled. The warm light of the morning sun flowed from the cracked house walls. In the windows were reflections of a cloudless sky. With some of the stolen coins, I bought a sausage at a butcher shop. We shared it. "Don't ever look at me like that again," I said to the dog, but I saw in his eyes that he did not understand. He was only a dog. He licked my fingers and kept his eye on the foot I'd kicked him with. For him, the foot was the danger. Not me. He no longer trusted the foot, this suspicious little cur. I liked him because he was my friend. The only friend I had.

In one place, there was a market. I walked off with a poncho, but someone noticed and shouted for the police.

"Stop that thief," a man yelled. "There he goes with his stinking dog."

We ran in between the market stands and a few people tried to stop me. I threw the poncho away and ran over a woman, who tried to grab me by the arm. The woman fell and turned over a table full of fake designer watches. I ran like a rabbit and was beginning to believe I had made it when, seemingly from nowhere, a police officer struck me on the shoulder with his club. It happened so suddenly that I could not dodge the blow. I felt something break in my shoulder, and the pain brought tears to my eyes. The police officer got behind me and pressed his club across my windpipe. He held it fast with both hands while he pushed his knee into my back. He choked me, cutting off my air with his club until I almost blacked out.

"If you make a move, I'll break your neck, you toad."

I didn't try anything. I couldn't. I could not even breathe. I just looked around for the dog, but he had disappeared. I saw the man from the stand where I had stolen the poncho. He was coming toward me with his fists swinging. His face was dark red, and he seethed with rage.

"That's him," he roared. "He's a thief. I'll bet he has money to pay for the poncho. They all have money, these little bastards."

On and on he went in his rage. My ears registered his voice, but I did not want to listen anymore. The lights went out, and the noise became softer and softer until it finally stopped.

*

I awoke because I had to pee. Slowly, clenching my teeth from the pain, I sat up. To my right was a door with iron bars. To the left, a set of bunk beds. On the lower bunk sat a man, staring at me. He wore pants full of holes and a dirty white undershirt stained from sweat. A cigarette hung from the corner of his mouth. The smoke crept up from his face to a small barred window high on the wall.

The man looked at me with dark, tired eyes.

"I have to pee," I said while I tried to stand up.

"You look like you've been living with dogs," said the man.

I pushed myself up to all fours and wrenched up what I had in my stomach. My body cramped, and I threw up the sausage and the blood I had swallowed. The man shouted for a captain. Captain Mendoza.

"I am trying to keep this cell clean," the man scolded. "Look around. Everything is tidy, dammit."

A man wearing a khaki uniform arrived. It was Captain Mendoza, a police officer. A golden badge stuck to his uniform shirt, a gold tooth and shifty eyes, in which I could see nothing but malice. He looked between the bars.

"What's going on here?" he said after staring at me for a moment.

"He is messing up the whole fuckin' cell," complained the man on the cot.

Captain Mendoza opened the door. Behind him was another police officer, who held a baton in his hands. Their badges sparkled like ornaments on a Christmas tree.

Once again, my mind turned to the photo. Papa Biddle, who showed up to give out small presents from the Red Cross to the children and the big Christmas tree behind the soccer goal. The colorful balloons hanging on it and the garlands and the little dolls made of straw and the men sitting in front of the bodega, studying my mother and my sister Theresa.

"He threw up?" the captain laughed. "You're lucky he didn't shit, you pig."

He came over to me and kicked me in the stomach. I doubled over on the floor into my vomit. He stood before me, his legs spread apart, his thumbs hooked in his belt. When I looked up, he spat in my face.

"Get up," he said.

I got up, surprised that I was able to do it.

"Outside," he said.

I went out. The man outside stuck the baton in my stomach.

"Wait," he said. I stood there.

Capitan Mendoza closed the cell door behind me. I waited, with my legs dangerously close to collapsing.

"Let's go," said the captain. "Forward."

They took me between them and brought me into a washroom. I had to undress, and they watched me as I took a cold shower, letting the water run over my head and my skinny body. As the water washed over my neck and my shoulder, where they had struck me and burned me, it stung my skin, and I tried not to wince.

"Wash your things," the captain ordered.

I saw in the shadows on the wall that the captain stepped behind me. I felt his hand on my back, and I felt his breath. I washed my pants out with soap and tried to rub the blood spots out of the material, attempting to ignore what I could feel on my back—the touch of his fingers on my wet skin. His breath on my neck where there was that burn, and his voice in my ears scaring the hell out of me.

"Come, little man," he said. "Blow me one."

His hand crept up the nape of my neck. He grabbed my hair and pulled my head back. I groaned from the pain. The man at the door laughed as Captain Mendoza's hand traveled over my chest and stomach. He grabbed me between the legs; he grabbed my penis, and he squeezed my balls so hard I went to my knees. He went down with me until I knelt on the floor. He stood up and pulled me around by the hair. I knelt before him in a puddle of water and soapsuds. We were still in the washroom. Somewhere, drops fell into a bucket. The man at the door had his teeth bared. His face was like an ugly mask. The captain let go of my hair.

"If you do it well, you can go," he said.

He began to unbutton his pants, and I drowned in his laugh echoing around the shower.

3
Don Fernando

"Boy," said the man, "what are you doing here?"

I was lying in the road in the middle of the night. A pickup truck's headlights blinded me.

The man helped me sit up.

"Is that your dog over there?" he asked.

I looked in the direction he was pointing. There lay the dog on the edge of the road. He peered across, his half-ear raised. I was so happy to see him again, I wanted to get up and hug him.

"Can you speak at all?"

I nodded.

"And you hear me?"

"Yes."

The man laughed. Then he just smiled.

"I am on my way home. Nobody else travels on this road. Not at this hour."

He gestured in the direction the headlights were pointing. The road was not a road. There were only long, deep wheel ruts with grass on either side. The grass stood knee high in the headlights, every stalk a curved line against the night sky.

"It is a bit more than six kilometers to Bosque Redondo Hacienda. There is nothing between here and there but the road and the night with its stars and the moon." He laughed again. "I do not know what Carmelita would say if I were to bring you and your dog home with me."

I sat up. "Who is Carmelita?" I asked.

"My daughter," he replied proudly. "I have fathered five daughters and three sons. Carmelita is the youngest. She was born six years ago."

I looked at him. He crouched next to me on the road, his

bright white shirt reflecting the headlights. He did not look like a haciendero, but more like a businessman from the city. He wore a red and blue striped necktie loosely around his neck. The top button of his shirt collar was open. On his left wrist, the gold of a watch glistened.

"What is your name, boy?" he asked.

"Santiago," I said.

"And where do you come from?"

I pointed out into the darkness with my head. From somewhere I wanted to say, but I did not. Somewhere, from where I once left to go to America. Somewhere, where my father got buried, and our land was still within the grasp of those it did not belong to, while the world no longer watched since no more shots got fired and no more soldiers died, and no villages got attacked, and no more blood was supposed to flow.

"You are not from the city, are you?"

"No."

"Where are you from, then?"

"Chiapas."

He nodded as if he already knew.

"Then, are you an Indian? A Tzotzil?"

"I am."

"And you are a Zapatista who gave up and ran away."

"My father was a Zapatista," I said. "He was a Zapatista, and he was my father and the father of my brothers and sisters."

"Was he a member of the group that called itself Las Abejas, the bees?"

I nodded. "Almost all the people in our village belonged to it. They are proud of being hardworking farmers."

"It is a political group that opposes the government. Sometimes the newspaper articles claim its connection to left-wing rebels."

I was silent.

"They say these rebels are communists. And terrorists."

I remained silent.

He laughed. "The newspapers write a lot," he said. "A piece of paper accepts everything without blushing. What happened to your father?"

"He was murdered."

"During the rebellion?"

"No. My father was murdered after everyone said no one else would get murdered."

"And now you are on your way to the United States, right? Because you have heard people live free and without fear in the United States of America."

"Yes."

He smiled. His teeth were as white as his shirt, and he wore a mustache close to his lip, narrow as a line.

"Can you handle horses, Santiago?"

I nodded. Back home, horses ran around like dogs. I could ride them all. Saddled or bareback, some even without bit and bridle.

"I will ask Pedro if he needs a helper," he said. "If he can use you, I will pay you a salary as a groom. It is not a lot, but I think you could well use the money. Your pockets are empty, right?"

"I don't own anything."

"Did you get robbed in the city?"

"Yes."

"The city is not a safe place. Not for a boy from Chiapas who does not know his way around. My son Ronaldo takes classes at the university in the city, but that is another world, a world that does not exist for people like you. Ronaldo often comes home over the weekends. He wants to become a politician, and once elected into the government clean out all corruption. He is young and filled with idealism and trust in a better future for Mexico. Ronaldo reminds me much of myself when I was a young student at law school. I wanted to wipe out poverty. Just like him. Poverty and corruption go hand in hand. My son Ronaldo will experience many disappointments in the course of his life, but perhaps he has the strength not to give up, even when everything seems futile."

I asked him for some water.

"I am sorry, kid, but I do not have any water with me. If you want to get up, I will help you. Then we will go home. There is a stream along the way with good water you can drink, and Luisa will put together a meal with something for you to drink when we get home."

He helped me to stand. It did not bother him to touch me, but I winced when he touched my shoulder.

"You hurt your shoulder?"

"Not as bad as I first thought. At first, it felt like something broke inside it."

"Does your mother know you are on the way to the United States?" he asked as he led me into the blinding lights of his car.

"Yes."

"Do you think the United States is a great country?"

It seemed he just wanted to keep my brain occupied, so I nodded.

"How about your mother? Does she think likewise?"

"She said I should go with God."

He smiled. "To God's Country?"

"Is there a country like that?" I asked him.

"That is a far-reaching question, Santiago, and I don't know the answer. I guess if you ever get there you will have to find out yourself."

The dog followed us to the truck.

"What is your dog's name?" he asked.

"He has no name," I said.

"Carmelita will give him a name."

He helped me get in. It was a new pickup, and it smelled like leather and his cologne inside. I leaned back into the seat, trying not to move my right shoulder too much.

There was soft music, some music that was foreign to me. The sound of angels, I guessed. Or the Devil's music. That depended probably on the pictures this music created in one's head. Next to me, between the driver's seat and mine, lay a telephone. At that time, I didn't know it was called a car phone. No one in Chiapas had a phone like this to call someone while driving. In the rearview mirror, I saw the man lift the dog up onto the truck bed, and the little dog curled up behind the passenger compartment and somehow stuck his nose between his two hind paws. He must have waited for me the entire time I was behind bars.

The man climbed in.

"By the way," he said, "I am Don Fernando Ochoa de Coronado. Sometimes my name is in the papers."

He picked up the telephone and punched in a number.

"Antonio, please tell Luisa I'm on my way home and that I'm bringing a guest."

He put the vehicle into first gear and drove, the telephone to his ear.

He laughed.

"No, Antonio. No need to alarm Silva. Everything is all okay. No, it is a boy. I picked him up on the road. He got robbed and beaten up."

He did not need to change gears; the pickup had an automatic transmission. I had no knowledge of such things, but later, he explained to me everything I needed to know, and much more.

"Yes, we will be home in twenty minutes," he said. And then: "Of course I know that it is after midnight, Antonio. It was a strenuous day."

He hung up.

"That was my second oldest son, Antonio. He was worried about me because I already called him at eleven as I was leaving the office."

He was silent for a while as he dwelt on his thoughts.

"I am a federal judge," he said finally. "That is why my name is sometimes in the papers."

We drove down the road.

"Surely, you do not read the papers."

The pickup shuddered and danced in the wheel furrows. I had to hold tight to the strap on the door.

"The road has been washed out by the winter rains," he said. "It rained a lot this year. Everything is green. The cattle have a lot to eat in the pastures. It will be a good year for the ranch. It will allow me to pay a horse-groom."

I stared out through the windshield. A coyote appeared in the headlights and immediately disappeared again.

"Don Coyote," he said. "There is not a cleverer animal than he, yet he walks into our traps again and again."

We crossed a stream bed that was almost dry. Don Fernando stopped, left the truck and collected water in his hands.

"Here, drink," he ordered me, and I bent over and drank out of his hands.

*

The lands of the Bosque Redondo Hacienda spread out over a broad valley with boundless pastures and a forested north slope. A road led in two or three long curves across a rocky ridge into the valley. In the headlights, I saw cows with calves in the meadows on both sides of the road. Some blocked our way, so Don Fernando had to sound the horn now and again to drive them off. Lights appeared, along with the dark outlines of large corrals that held dozens of horses.

The hacienda itself consisted of several buildings. One of them was the main house, a massive white block within an enclosure wall, an enormous arched gateway and what looked to be a watchtower. The other buildings, Don Fernando, explained to me, were stables and storage for machinery and tools. Also, there were several smaller houses where vaqueros lived, a bunk house with a dining hall and a kitchen and the supervisor's house. His name was Raul Viera, and he had a family. Pedro Legarra, who was in charge of the horses, lived in a room in the barn because he could never sleep well in a place not smelling of horses.

It was just past midnight when we arrived. Lights were on everywhere and parts of the hacienda and its immediate surroundings were lit up nearly as bright as day. Also, I saw a man moving in that tower, holding a semi-automatic rifle.

"They have been waiting for my return," said Don Fernando. "Before, when I did not yet have a telephone in my car, I never would drive alone at such a late hour. The man there in the tower, he would accompany me as my bodyguard wherever I went. His name is Señor Silva. You will meet him."

He stopped in front of the main house, which had a veranda with a tile roof supported by thick white columns. Stairs led up to the veranda. As soon as he stopped the pickup, a man appeared from somewhere and opened the door for him.

Don Fernando stepped out and came around the pickup and opened my door. When I climbed out, he wanted to take me by the arm and support me, but I said I did not need any help. He smiled and let me get out on my own.

The dog in the bed of the pickup stayed there; I guess he slept during the drive despite the bumpy road. Now he looked at me and then he looked at the people on the veranda, standing in the warm light of some lamps. I wondered why he didn't jump out of the truck bed.

"Carmelita, my dear, shouldn't you have been in bed long ago?" Don Fernando called to a girl standing at the top of the steps in an ankle-length nightshirt.

"I was asleep, but then I woke up," a soft voice answered. "Who have you brought with you, Papa?"

He turned to me. "Come," he said. "Midnight is as good a time as any to meet my family."

I looked back at the dog. The dog just watched everything that was going on. He seemed to be a smart dog. Smarter than most people. As the man who had opened the door for Don Fernando approached him, he ducked. The man told him he would take care of him. "You are hungry, and you need a bath," he said. The dog jumped out and followed the man into a shed. As they came out, the dog wore a collar. He followed the man to a dog house and did not mind as the man chained him and filled a bowl with water and another with food he got out of the shed.

"Paco, our old dog just died a few weeks ago," Don Fernando explained to me smiling. "I promised Carmelita to get another dog."

He was very proud of his family. As I later learned, he held his head high because he led a content and happy life, although his wife had died at Carmelita's birth.

The man who had opened the door for Don Fernando drove the pickup into a garage. Up in the tower, the man with the rifle leaned out over the balustrade.

"Everything okay, patrón?" he called.

"Everything is all right, Umberto," the haciendero called

up to him. "Our guest is a boy from Chiapas who got robbed in the city."

"I will look at him closely tomorrow," the man called back. "A boy from Chiapas could be a poisonous snake."

The haciendero laughed and went up the steps in front of me. His daughter Carmelita hugged him, and he kissed her and she kissed him. A young woman stood in the doorway; her black hair was combed back tightly and tied in a knot. She looked at me distrustfully with her dark eyes.

"This is Carmelita," he said, taking the young girl by the hand, and drawing my attention back to her. "And there is Luisa, my eldest daughter. Without her, the family would be hopelessly lost." He pointed to the young man. "Antonio, this boy has run into difficulties. I hope he will stay with us a while. He knows horses."

"Good for him," Antonio said.

The haciendero laughed again. He seemed to do this often. "Antonio, my son, trusts nobody whom he does not know. And that is okay. We live in a strange time when, unfortunately, a person has to be precautious to turn his back on anyone. I do not know if it really was different in earlier times, but, if my memory does not deceive me, I grew up without fear. Of course, I was afraid of ghosts, but nothing else." He embraced Luisa.

"Your supper is on the table," said Luisa. "Perhaps I should have his brought to him in the bunkhouse."

"No, not at all, precious. He will not be living with our vaqueros; he will stay with us at our home. We will let him stay in one of the guest rooms, like a private guest and a friend of our family. And when the opportunity arises, he will also eat with us. Only if he prefers to stay at the bunkhouse, he is free to do so."

"And how, if I may ask, has he earned the honor to become

part of our family?" Antonio asked. "You just said you have never seen him before."

His father put an arm around his son's shoulders and pulled him close.

"This boy comes from far away, my son, where people have to fight for their right to live free," he said. "He is seeking his way north. For any kid less fortunate than mine it is a challenging path with many obstacles, temptations, and traps. I do not know if he will one day reach his destination, which is, by the way, the US of A, but here, at the Hacienda Redondo, he is to feel as secure as if your mother were here with us, Antonio."

Antonio said nothing more. He seemed to know it would be pointless. His father had decided, and that was that.

Luisa led us into the house. On a nicely set table, under a gigantic chandelier, was my supper on a porcelain plate. I ate with silver cutlery and drank ice water from a crystal glass. I had never done such things before, never sat at a table decorated like this. Insecure and nervous as I was, I struck my teeth with the fork, and the food fell back onto the plate halfway to my mouth. The haciendero sat at the head of the table and read a newspaper. He probably was reading that newspaper only to give me the feeling nobody would watch me.

"I hope it does not bother you if I read the paper while you are eating?" he asked me.

I shook my head. Luisa watched me while I ate. I was careful not to strike the silverware against the porcelain plate and not to slurp when I sipped water out of the fancy glass. There were potatoes and pieces of chicken and beans. Fresh tortillas made of corn meal. I ate everything. I was hungry as a bear, and I wanted to get rid of the nasty feeling I had before I fainted in the road. I did not know why I had lost consciousness.

Never in my life had I felt as lousy as after they had kicked me—literally—from the jail. Anger and pain made me nearly collapse in front of the prison gate, but I forced myself to run, simply to be away from that place and those two men. While I ran through the night without knowing where to hide, I only thought of going back and killing those two bastards who had abused me. But I had neither a knife nor a pistol, and my machete, which I knew how to use well, had been stolen.

When I had finally collapsed, it was as if I suddenly did not have any bones in my body. I just fell to the ground, and I was sick. I threw up as if wrenching my stomach from my body until I knew I had nothing more. The next thing I was aware of was the man in the headlights, the haciendero.

His daughter wanted to know why I was on that road, which led only to the hacienda and not on the main highway going north.

"I did not know where that road led," I said.

"You did not know the road would end here, at the hacienda?"

"No. I did not even know it was a road. I simply was going."

She studied me. I continued eating. She studied me, because, just like her brother, she did not trust me. She certainly would not have turned her back on me.

Her father leafed through the newspaper.

"The people who robbed you, did they chase after you?" Luisa asked.

"No."

"And your injuries, did they come from them?"

"Yes."

"Were they street bandits?"

"They were some boys and a girl."

"A gang?"

"Yes."

She nodded and studied me further as I ate. I had some trouble lifting my right arm.

"There are many such gangs in the city. Street gangs. They terrorize honest people. Could it be that you belonged to such a group of kids and got into trouble because of it?"

I put down my fork and knife and wiped my mouth with the back of my hand.

"For that, one uses a napkin," Luisa said and pointed to a rolled up piece of thick material lying next to my plate. It was held together by an ornamented silver ring. Feeling with my tongue that my mouth was clean, I wiped the back of my hand on the napkin.

"Santiago is from Chiapas," said Don Fernando without lowering his newspaper. "Here it reads that conditions in Chiapas have not improved, and the Indians are going to renew their rebellion against the government. The report comes from San Cristóbal de las Casas."

San Cristóbal de las Casas. When my grandmother was still alive, we sold wicker baskets and mats at the market in that city. She and Mother wove them. We sold corn too when there was a good harvest, and stores of corn and beans in the village were enough to last until the next harvest. San Cristóbal de las Casas was the city where I was almost run over by a truck when I ran across the street to look at a man with a barrel organ and a capuchin on a chain. Since leaving, I had received no information from home. The people I came in contact with did not know what was happening in Chiapas. The rebellion was long over, they had said. Everything was once again in order. Damned Indio's, they also said. If they brought about a devaluation of the peso with their rebellion, then the entire country would have to suffer.

"Here. In the La Jornada newspaper, it reads: On the

fourteenth of March, in the Indian village of San Pedro Nixtal'ucum, four Indian peasant farmers were killed in a battle between the police and Tzotzil Indians. Several rebels and some police officers were wounded. Over three hundred fifty people fled their huts and sought refuge in a nearby village. The police have arrested a few dozen people, mainly sympathizers of the Zapatista National Liberation Army. Shots were fired at the rebels from a government helicopter after they once again attacked the state police unit just as it was leaving the village with the prisoners."

Don Fernando looked up from the newspaper.

"Those are your people, Santiago, is that not so?" He placed the open paper on the table and pushed it over to me. There were two pictures on one page that appeared familiar to me. State police threatened a family with machine guns. A house burned in the background. In the other picture, the Governor of Chiapas. I read the caption. "Battles between police and rebels disturb the peace process in Chiapas."

"You can read, Santiago?" the haciendero wondered.

"Yes. For a while, there was a school in our village. Every morning, we all went to school, where we learned to read, write and do calculations. Then, one morning, when we came to school, the door was bolted, and Señor Gonzalez did not come to unlock it for us."

"Why not?"

"He could not."

"He could not?"

"They had come for him in the night."

"Who came for him?"

"The police."

"Why?"

"They claimed he was teaching us communist ideas, but all of us knew he never did that. To us, Señor Gonzalez was nothing more than an excellent teacher. They also said that, in any case, there was no more money for schools and education."

"That is a disgrace, Santiago. But in this aspect, the rebellion seems to have accomplished something. It says in his article that schools are being established in the villages again. And, Santiago, it seems, at last, some people all over the world have become aware of the injustices in Chiapas."

I did not answer as I stared at the newspaper on the table.

"If you want to know the world as it is, read the papers, Santiago. Everything is right there, the truth and also all the lies. The good and the bad."

He got up from his chair.

"Come, I will show you your room and where you can shower. Luisa will get clothes for you tomorrow, right, Luisa? Santiago needs a shirt and pants and a pair of boots. Santiago, no sooner as you get outfitted, report to Pedro. It will not be hard for you to find him. Wherever the horses are, there you will find Pedro. Also, I think that Señor Silva wants to put a few questions to you. He is responsible for my security and the security of my family."

I thanked Luisa for the meal, and I followed her father out through the hall and up the steps. The family bedrooms were up on the second floor. The guest rooms were one level higher, right under the tile roof. He showed me to an elegantly furnished room.

"It is the roomiest guest room we have," he said. "The door there leads directly into a bathroom." He opened the door and turned on the light in the bathroom. I saw myself and him in the mirror, and I was shocked when I saw my reflection. It was not me, but rather a strange boy who stared back like an evil ghost. It was a frightened boy with a blood-smeared, swollen face with eyes that glowed full of hatred.

"You will feel better tomorrow," Don Fernando's reflection said to me. "Rest now. The day after tomorrow is Sunday and, as always, I will take a horseback ride. If you would like, you can accompany Carmelita and me. And perhaps Antonio will come along, although riding is not enjoyable for him."

He went to the door, then turned around once again.

"I hope you like it here with us," he said. "Enjoy your stay, Santiago. Try to get rid of your painful memories and your hatred. It's one thing to be hurt, another yet to let anger destroy you."

"Thank you," I said. I had not often used these words, and it made me uneasy to hear them coming from my mouth.

"Good night," said Don Fernando.

"Good night," I answered.

He went out, closing the door quietly behind him. I sat down on the edge of the bed and stared at the photo on the wall—the photo on the wall at home. I saw my mother's face and Papa Biddle's nose and my little sister Paolita. I saw my father as they killed him. I saw how they put a bullet in his head. Just like that, and only because he threatened them with his fist and told them that the land here was the land of his fathers and not the land of the government. He had stood up to them in his own house, where he'd felt so secure he no longer thought it was necessary to have a single bullet in his hunting rifle. It hung by its shoulder strap on the post, right next to the Polaroid photo. There, they killed him. As he lay on the floor and could hear nothing more, an officer bent down and grabbed him by the ear and said: "Listen up, you damned Zapatista. This land is Mexico, and whoever says Mexico is Indian land will find himself very much mistaken."

That was the day when my mother packed our things, and we went to the village and into the small hut where my grandmother lived. A short time later, my grandmother died of grief over my father's death.

I sat for a long time on the edge of the bed, lost in my sorrow. Then I went into shower in the bathroom and let warm water run over me. At my feet, in the white tub, a puddle of water, blood, and dirt formed. Before I went to bed, I cleaned the tub, but it didn't seem as dazzlingly white as it had been before. I hung the bath towel on the rack, combed my hair and went back into the guest room. I looked around a while to memorize everything in case I woke in the night and forgot where I was. Then I put out the light, but the pain kept me awake. I looked out the window at the brightly lit courtyard below. At the gate stood a man with a rifle. I could not make out whether it was the same man I had seen in the tower, this Señor Silva.

I looked across the yard to the dog house. The little dog slept all curled up. His fur yet to be bathed.

4
Silva

Silva came across the front yard to tell Carmelita he wanted to speak with me in private. Neither one of us saw where he had come from. A few steps from us, he halted, and asked Carmelita to leave.

Carmelita looked at him and then at me. I gave her the little dog, which I had in my arms.

"Please go," I said to her.

She hesitated. Then she looked at Señor Silva once more, who forced an odd smile.

"Just go. I will not harm him, Carmelita."

She did not say a word and went into the house. As the screen door closed behind her, he turned away from me and said that I should step out from the shadow of the house and into the sunlight.

I stepped into the glaring sunlight so he could see me better. He stayed in the shade, his thumbs hooked in his holster that held a revolver. He paced back and forth in the shadow of the house, only a few steps, without looking at me.

Although he did not look like the captain at the prison, he reminded me of him. He looked hardened. Like a man who has fought for his power and does not shrink back from misusing it. When he abruptly stopped and turned toward me, he looked at me as if he were waiting for me to drop to my knees before him.

"Do you know who I am?" he asked.

I nodded, squinting in the sunlight.

"My name is Silva. The people here call me Señor Silva."

He wanted a response, but I couldn't think of anything to say. So, I remained silent.

"They tell me you come from Chiapas."

"Yes."

"Do you have a family?"

I shook my head.

"You have no family?"

"No."

"No father?"

"No."

"And no mother?"

"I have a mother."

"Then you are not an orphan?"

"No."

"Do you have brothers and sisters?"

"Yes."

"Did they stay with your mother?"

"No. Two of my brothers and one of my sisters are gone."

"Gone?"

"They were adopted."

"You do not know where they are?"

"No. Only Miguelito is still at home."

"Where is that? Home?"

"Los Chorros."

"That's an Indian village, right?"

I nodded.

"Why did you leave?"

"My father got killed by soldiers."

"During the rebellion in January?"

"No, he was killed later."

"Later? You mean he was not one of the one hundred forty-five who died during the rebellion?"

"No. They murdered him at home."

"Government soldiers?"

"Yes."

"I did not read anything about it in the newspapers."

I bowed my head.

"Look me in the eye, boy. When I talk to you, look me in the eye."

I tried to look him in the eye, but I couldn't.

"It was just by chance that you collapsed on the road leading here?"

"Yes."

"I don't believe that."

"It is true, though."

"Look me in the eye."

I raised my head. I looked him in the eye. His gaze forced its way into me and rummaged around in me. I wanted to kill him at that moment, the desire burned within me, but I did not know how. I had nothing to kill him with. Not even my machete I could have used to cut off his head with one swing.

"Good," he said finally. "You can go. Pedro is waiting for you."

I walked across the yard. My shoulder still hurt, but not as bad as yesterday.

Carmelita, along with the little dog, rushed out of the house and across the yard to the stables. The dog was soaking wet, and soap spuds flew from his ears. Luisa came out of the house to the edge of the veranda. "Not in the house, Carmelita," she called after her younger sister. "You'll have to clean up your bathroom later, you hear me?"

Over at the stables, Pedro was busy currying a horse. He was a small man with a wrinkled face and a stiff leg. I would learn later that one of the horses had kicked him in the knee a few years prior.

The horse Pedro curried was a tall beautiful gelding with a shiny copper-colored coat and white stockings on its forelegs. The dog ran between Carmelita's legs. She fell, and the little dog and the girl turned into a yelping and screeching tangle in the dust. I went across the plaza, and the dog saw me there, and he came to me. He smelled of shampoo. Carmelita struggled back onto her feet and beat the dust out of her T-shirt and blue jeans. With her hair cut short and her bangs, she almost looked like a boy.

"What is the dog's name?" she called.

"He has no name," I said. She came to me and tagged along behind me.

"Do you want him to have a name?" she asked.

"Do you have anything in mind?"

"Rata."

"Rata?"

"Yes. It is a name that fits. When he is all wet he looks more like a giant rat than a dog."

I had to laugh. "That's right," I said. "He really does look like a giant rat."

"Except for his legs and his tail."

"Not his tail?"

"No. Have you never seen a rat's tail?"

"Sure. I even ate one once."

She stared at me. "You are lying."

"No. Why should I do that?"

"You are lying all the same."

"If you think I'm lying, it's impossible for me to make you believe me."

"Then tell me why you would have to eat a rat's tail?"

"That was when we went to live with my grandmother in the village. There was very little to eat, and so we caught rats and ate them."

She fell into a thoughtful silence. Then Pedro noticed us.

"This is Santiago," said Carmelita. "He is supposed to help you with the horses."

"And who are you, child?" Pedro asked.

"Me? Do you not know me? I'm Carmelita." She struck a pose and grinned at him impudently.

"Really," he said and put his hand to his forehead. "You must have grown a whole lot again overnight."

*

From that day on, I helped Pedro with the horses. I almost forgot my original plan to not stay at the hacienda for long.

The horses Don Fernando owned were first class, and he was nearly as proud of his horse breeding as he was of his family and his post as a federal judge.

"Many have already tried to buy me," he told me once while glancing over the edge of his newspaper. "Some have offered me lots of money for small favors, others had promised me a career in politics, but my family gave me the strength to resist all their attempts."

During the week, I seldom saw him. Most of the time, he left the house quite early in the morning. Sometimes, I would see him from a distance, driving his pickup through the gray morning mist. Sometimes, he stopped at the corrals and looked at the horses, full of admiration and affection; he would speak with Pedro about this or that horse. Mainly he spent the entire day in the city and came home after dark. He often stayed in town, then telephoned and spoke with Luisa, Carmelita and Antonio. His other children were all away. Ronaldo went to the University. Federico, the youngest of his three sons, was an exchange student in Madrid. Dolores, his second oldest daughter, worked for an airline in Florida, Belinda was a dance instructor in Guadalajara and Selina was married and lived with her family in Monterey, where her husband had a legal firm. Even though, until now, I had never had anything to do with people like Don Fernando and his family, I realized that the haciendero was an extraordinary man—one who appeared like a rock to me, while I drifted helplessly in a storm-swept sea. I would have only had to cling on to him, but I simply did not have the strength.

"There are some holidays during the year when all my children come back home," he said during a Sunday ride. We had stopped the horses on a hill and looked down the valley and into the distant forest and chain of hills. An airplane left a white streak in the blue sky. "At Christmas and Easter they all come here, and we celebrate together. Then there is another special day. My wife's birthday. It is in October. The twentieth. Every year on that day, everybody comes back, and we celebrate the memory of a wonderful woman who is my great and only love."

He told me about her as if I was his best friend, and perhaps I actually was at that moment. He told me of the day when they first met, and he showed me pictures of their wedding, and of a trip to Europe. When he stopped talking, his thoughts were far away and in a time when I did not exist. When he returned and noticed me, he was surprised. He smiled and told me he had never told all that to anyone before. I think this surprised him.

Every Sunday, the excursion led us across his land and up to the hill where his wife's grave was—next to her mother's and father's graves and next to their son, who had lost his life in a motorcycle accident. We rode together through the woods, and he told me of his life. I listened to him carefully, and I read the words from his lips when his voice became so soft I could not understand him otherwise. We rode through the open valley to a lake. There, we reigned the horses and would remain sitting on them, looking out into the vast landscape where his cattle grazed. We rode the borders of his land; we talked with his neighbors and with the people in a little village called San Miguel, and the people were surprised by his companion, a boy from Chiapas whom he had taken into his family as if he were a long-lost son.

Sometimes Carmelita went with us on her pinto pony, and Rata ran behind us, scaring up rabbits and quail from the brush, which he chased, barking until his tongue hung so far out of his mouth he could have almost stepped on it with his front paws.

The days I spent at Bosque Redondo Hacienda were good ones. Good days, because my wounds healed and, for the first time in a long while, I almost had the feeling I belonged to somebody, and Don Fernando's family was also my family. His land was my land, and his life was my life. He was an odd man who awakened an odd feeling in me I had never sensed before. I had no name for it, and so I asked Pedro about it.

"You respect him," said Pedro. "Just like everybody here. Me too. I respect him because he is a respectable man. Open and honest and reliable. I do not know anybody else like him. It is a shame that he loves a woman who is dead for so long."

"To him she is alive," I said.

"Why do you say that?" he asked.

"Because I have seen her with my own eyes," I replied. Pedro looked at me and shook his head. I don't think he understood what I had said, but he believed me anyway.

If I had let myself go, I could have nearly become another person there on the hacienda. My wounds healed. I had dreams like I had never dreamt before, and sometimes when I woke I forgot where I really was.

Down deep in myself, I again sensed the fire roaring in my heart, the way it had in prison for the first time since my father's death.

"What are your goals?" the haciendero asked me one day.

I could not give him an answer.

"Then tell me your dreams, Santiago," he urged.

"I have no dreams," I lied to him.

"But it is important for a young person to have dreams and to set a goal. A point on the horizon he knows he can reach."

My father had once told me the same thing, but now I laughed because my father had not had the chance to set his eye on a goal. It was before he had connected with the Zapatistas.

"Without a goal, you will wander through a life that passes much too quickly," Don Fernando continued. "Santiago, my family was not wealthy. I had to work hard to finance my education. I met my wife, Consuela, at the University. Her parents owned this hacienda, and they did not want her to get involved with me, not with a poor wretch who was trying to be a lawyer. I showed them. I not only became a lawyer, but I also became a judge. Nobody could stop me from following my path and reaching my goal."

I asked him whether he had already reached his goal.

"When I close my eyes for good, then I will be at my goal," he said. He was an odd man. Every evening, he read to me from the newspaper, although he noticed that I hadn't developed much interest in it—learning whatever about whichever event—it was all foreign to me. War in the Balkans. I had no idea where that was. Somewhere on the other side of the world. A conference at the United Nations where they discussed global warming.

I listened to him and was bored. Somehow, I realized that politicians lied a lot to lead us quite nicely around by the nose. They did not work for us as they were supposed to. They made laws that did not seem to help us much with our daily lives. On the contrary, most of them hindered us from living in peace and becoming prosperous. They made sure the rich got richer, while the poor had less and less. They stocked up their police force and their military in case we rebelled against the injustices we felt but could not name. Everything had to do with money. Money was power and anyone who did not have it was out of luck. While listening to him with one ear, I dreamt of being a rich man. Like him. One who, above all, could be proud of what he had accomplished.

He never urged me to read the newspaper myself. Or to read a book. In his study, you could scarcely see the wall with all the books weighing down the sturdy shelves. Right up to the ceiling. Others lay on his desk and on a chest of drawers, and some even on the floor next to the leather sofa and lamp.

Sometimes he would call me into his study when he knew I was in the house, in my room lying on my bed and staring at the ceiling.

"Here is something that will also interest you," he said when I took a seat in his study. Surrounded by books and in the silence ruling this room, I felt lost.

He didn't understand that I had put behind me whatever might hinder me on my path to the future. I didn't want to hear anything more about political injustice and the struggles of the poor and starving. I had heard it all from my father and those who had fought with him. I had experienced it myself when the soldiers marched into our village and treated us like troublesome pests to be destroyed before we multiplied.

He read me the peace negotiations taking place in one of the villages in Chiapas—the government had taken the upper hand for the first time, because our people were not united. Fewer and fewer of them believed that the January Revolution, which lasted twelve days and cost the lives of many men, women, and children, could heal the wounds inflicted on my people through centuries of exploitation and persecution.

He lay the paper on the table and looked at me as if trying to determine whether I had been listening.

"Santiago?"

"Yes?"

"Pedro told me you are thinking of leaving the hacienda."

"How does Pedro know that? We never spoke about staying or leaving."

"Pedro knows you, Santiago." He looked at me. "Let me ask you directly: Is it true that you have it in mind to leave?"

"Yes, it's true."

He smiled, but it was not the smile that I was accustomed to seeing from him.

"Of course, you know that you are like a son to me, and that you can stay here as long as you want."

"I know that."

"But you have decided against it. True? Do you not feel at home with us?"

I shook my head. "No, it's not that. It's just that I remember I was on my way to the North before I came here."

"Are you saying that because you do not want to hurt my feelings?"

"I cannot stay here."

"Why not?"

"Because I once had a goal. And because there are things to take care of."

"Was it a goal worth the striving?"

"I don't know."

"But you don't want to talk to me about it, right?"

"Yes."

"Then tell me, what are these things that are so urgent?"

"Things I don't want to talk about."

"If you tell me what is oppressing you, perhaps I could stand at your side."

I didn't tell him. How could I have? I was still burdened with hatred. How could I have told him about the terror of waking up in the middle of the night because I had dreamt of killing the captain in Mexico City? I had killed him a thousand times. A thousand times, I saw him on his knees begging for mercy, but I had no pity for him. For all he did to me, and perhaps to others before me, I punished him with a bullet in his head. That would be my vengeance. It was what I had to do.

"Tell me in time when you decide to leave the hacienda, Santiago," he said.

I promised him he would be the first to know.

He smiled, stood up and came around the table. He lay his hand on my shoulder.

"I hope you'll reach your destination, Santiago," he said.

Realizing he was certain I would leave, I sat paralyzed in my chair.

"I am sure your dreams will be fulfilled, and that's what I'll focus on when you're no longer here with us. Then I can tell myself you're on the right path, Santiago."

He hugged me and kissed me on the cheek. Then he went out and left me there alone. He had never done that before. It had always been me who had left while he stayed at his desk. I heard his steps in the hall, and I heard him speaking quietly with Luisa. I was about to leave when my glance fell onto a picture in the newspaper. In the photo, he sat before a dark wall near a painting. His face appeared pale. Part of a flag close to the right margin. Don Fernando supported himself with his left hand on a desk. He wore a dark robe, with only part of his collar and the knot of his necktie visible.

I had no trouble reading the title.

"THE IRON JUDGE" was printed there in bold letters, and under that headline in smaller letters: "Judge Fernando Ochoa in legal action against Miguel Saldivar-Otero."

Because it would have taken me at least two or three hours

to read the entire article, I got up and went outside. Near the shed, Carmelita was giving Rata a bubble bath in a tub. When the dog saw me coming out of the house, and that Carmelita was distracted, he used the opportunity to race across the plaza like a scorched piglet, shaking green foam off his coat then throwing himself into a mud puddle by the creek.

"Your fault," Carmelita shouted at me. "Now he smells like a horse again."

"He would rather smell like a horse than like a sour apple," I said, pointing at the shampoo bottle with a green apple on the label.

*

Silva practiced shooting. He did it twice every week, usually on Tuesdays and Thursdays. Carmelita and I watched him sometimes from a safe distance. His shooting range was a hollow on the other side of a wide, dried-out creek bed. With a bulldozer, he had thrown up a mound of sand and gravel for a bullet-stop. He put up targets in the form of people, with torsos and heads, but without arms and legs. He shot at these targets with every weapon in his arsenal. With automatic pistols and revolvers, with small machine guns and a variety of rifles and shotguns. Usually, Carmelita held her ears with both hands, especially when he fired off a staccato of shots with the submachine guns, or when he shredded a target with a shotgun load. And Rata never ventured anywhere near the hollow. As soon as he saw Silva cross the plaza to his pickup with his weapons, he would hide in the horse barn under a pile of old bedding straw. Silva's training lasted at least three or four hours.

He shot from various positions; lying on the ground, kneeling, sitting, standing, with his back to the target, from a quick spin, rolling on the ground, from a racing dive onto an old mattress and running from every position twice, three times, sometimes more. Once, he even stood on his head and shot a target right in the middle of the chest.

"Silva is a fantastic shot," Carmelita said, reaching into a bag for some ear protectors Silva had brought along. She gave me a pair and put on hers. "You got to wear these, otherwise, by this evening, you might be deaf." She pointed at Silva. "Look at him; he is the best shot I know. He could shoot out the eye of a fly."

"Poor fly," I said and put on the ear protectors.

"Can you shoot?" she asked, her voice muffled.

"I have never tried," I answered loudly.

"You have never shot a gun?"

"No. Have you?"

"Sure. Many times. Silva said I was a natural."

"You? Probably it will scarcely ever be necessary for you to shoot the eye out of a fly, Carmelita."

We crossed the streambed, and we approached him cautiously. He saw us coming and stopped shooting. The air in the hollow smelled of gunpowder. My ears rang.

"Señor Silva, can you imagine? Santiago has never shot a gun," she blurted out. "I bet I can do better than he can. Could we shoot a little at those targets over there?"

The shadow of the bill of his cap lay across Silva's face. He wore sunglasses with mirrored lenses and large blue headphones.

"Could we, Señor Silva?" asked Carmelita once again.

Silva looked at me. "You have never shot a gun, boy?"

I shook my head.

"Down there in Chiapas, they are fighting there? The Indians fight the government soldiers?"

"My father fought."

"I thought you did not have a father."

"My father is dead."

He cocked his head and looked at me as if he had not heard right.

"Your father is dead?"

"Yes. Government soldiers shot him."

Now he took the ear protectors off his head. "How did that happen?"

"They came to our home and shot him."

"He had no rifle? Or a pistol?"

"He had an old hunting rifle, unloaded at the time."

"His rifle was not loaded?"

"Yes."

"Why was it not loaded?"

"Because he had no money to buy bullets."

Silva bared his teeth. "An unloaded rifle is pretty much worthless if you need to defend your life. Come here, both of you. I will show you how to handle this small but effective weapon."

He took the magazine out of the submachine gun. Then he had Carmelita hold the weapon, and I was surprised she could even operate the trigger.

"You see, like that. It doesn't do anything," he explained, facing me. "If you have to use an unloaded rifle to defend yourself I advise you to use it as a club." He took it from Carmelita and gave it to me.

"This is how you hold it: with the buttstock on your bicep, directly under your shoulder. Put your left hand on this grip here. That way you can fire off a volley even when you have to move at the same time. Would you like to give it a try?"

I almost shit my pants, but I didn't let it show. My heart wanted to burst. I'd never held a submachine gun in my hands, let alone fired one.

"With this little wonder, your father might have had a chance, boy," Silva said.

I shook my head. "He did not know they would come to kill him. Not to his house."

He smiled and took the gun from me. Expertly, he shoved a full magazine into the loading chamber and released the safety.

"Are you ready?" he asked both of us, and just as I adjusted my headphones, the gun in his hands barked angrily, and more than a dozen bullets tore through one of the targets and burrowed into the backstop. It lasted only two or three seconds. No more. One short burst and the magazine was half empty. A haze of blue smoke moved with the wind.

"Imagine, those were the soldiers," he said to me. "Here, boy, but be careful. The thing almost shoots itself as soon as you touch that trigger."

I took the gun and held it as he had shown me. I stretched out my trigger finger until I was next to Silva, facing the target.

"Lean a little bit forward," he said. "As if you had to march into the wind with the gun in a firing position. And think about it; when you fire off a series, the action pulls the muzzle upward. That means you have to grip it firmly and hold steady against that kickback."

The sweat ran into my eyes. I stared at the target, and I saw the captain in the shower kneeling in front of me on the ground. My blood turned cold. Gently, I placed my finger on the trigger. I had scarcely touched it when the little submachine gun roared. I felt how it wanted to jump out of my hands, and more from shock than kickback, I tumbled backward as if a horse had kicked me in the chest. There I sat in the gravel with the sting of burnt powder in my nose and the echo of the shots in my head.

Silva, whom I had never seen laugh before, was doubled over. Carmelita was screaming bloody murder because she thought I had shot myself in the stomach.

"Stop screaming," I grumbled. Silva helped me up and suggested I show Carmelita I wasn't riddled with bullets. I danced around her in a circle. "Look. No holes anywhere. Not a drop of blood."

"He hit the target, Carmelita," said Silva, taking the gun out of my hands. "For a beginner, he is a fair shot. Now it's your turn, Carmelita."

"Me? Not with that thing. I want the same pistol as last time."

Silva gave her a .25 caliber automatic and, after one miss, she put three shots through the target. He congratulated her, and she looked at me proudly.

"What do you say, Santiago?"

"You're very skilled," I said. It made her even prouder. She walked around with the gun in her hand, and Silva had to remind her to lock it.

I asked whether he would let me shoot with one of the revolvers. He reached for a .38 special with a mother-of-pearl grip. "Supposedly, this once belonged to the famous revolutionary Emiliano Zapata," he said. "You must know who this man is?"

"A hero," I said.

"He lived a hundred years ago," he said. "Your people in Chiapas call themselves Zapatistas in his honor."

"My father was a Zapatista."

He handed me the weapon.

"Keep your finger off the trigger as long as you are not ready to shoot, boy. Do you see those three cans over there on the embankment?"

"Yes."

"You have six bullets in the cylinder. If you shoot all three cans off the embankment, I will give you this beautiful revolver for the time you are here."

I wanted to look him in the eyes, but I simply couldn't do it. Something in his eyes irritated me. Made me unsure.

He laughed. "Six shots, boy. From the stance and location where you' are standing now. It's less than twenty steps to the embankment."

I looked at the embankment. Even if it were only twenty steps, the cans looked small from where I was.

"Even I could hit them," Carmelita laughed, "with the automatic."

"If he leaves one standing, then you're on, Carmelita," Silva promised.

I raised the revolver with both hands and pulled back the hammer. Carefully, I put my finger on the trigger. I closed one eye tightly and took aim with the other. My hands began to shake. I scarcely brought the front and back sights into line.

"Aim at the bottom of the can," I heard Silva say. I tried to squeeze the trigger, but the hammer did not fall. My finger had cramped on the trigger and did not want to move. My arms were getting tired, and I noticed I was aiming lower and lower. "Start over," Silva ordered, adjusting his earmuffs.

I dropped my arms until the barrel pointed at the ground.

I had held my breath the whole time. When my lungs almost burst, I exhaled strongly and breathed deeply a few times.

"Should I show you how it goes?" Carmelita asked.

"You can show me how to burp a doll," I said.

"I don't play with dolls," she said.

"Why not?"

"Because I'm not a girl."

"But you are a girl."

"No. It only looks that way. Ask Señor Silva. He has known me a lot longer, thank you."

"That is so," said Silva and he winked at me so Carmelita could not see it. "She is not a girl. She is a kid."

"Now you know." Carmelita tugged at my shirt. "I'm a kid."

"Yes. Now I know," I said. With slightly bent arms, I raised the revolver until I could see the first can over the front and the back sight. Without hesitating another second, I squeezed the trigger and, to my surprise, the can flew in the air as if there were a frog inside. It fell about three or four meters back onto the gravel and rolled down a slope.

"You hit," Carmelita shouted and clapped her hands. "You hit it, Santiago."

"Now the second one," said Silva.

I raised the revolver, fired and hit again.

"You hit!" Carmelita shouted.

"You can't do it a third time," said Silva. I knew he wanted to throw me off, but my tunnel vision had kicked in by this point.

"Want to bet?"

"Bet on wat?

"That I hit the can."

"With the next shot?"

"Yes, with the next shot."

"From where you're standing?"

"Yes, from here."

"How much?"

"A thousand pesos."

"One thousand pesos?"

"Yes."

"Bueno. I will give you one thousand pesos if you hit it. But if not…"

I raised the revolver, took aim and squeezed before he could finish his sentence. "A thousand pesos," I said into the echo of the shot.

He stared at where the can had stood and didn't say a word.

5
Mendoza

I left the hacienda on a Monday night without telling anyone. I didn't even say good-bye to the dog. He got up, stretched himself and came toward me until the chain stopped him.

It was a moonless night. The sky was overcast. Lightning flashed on the southeast horizon, sharply illuminating the outline of the hills. A fresh wind blew through the valley. Dust swirled, lifted by the horses' hooves as they moved about nervously in the corrals, startled by the distant rumbling.

At dawn, I wanted to be in the city. I had the clothes and money Don Fernando had given to me, the thousand pesos from Silva, and a small revolver, which I had found lying in a box in the shed.

Fortunately, Rata wasn't much of a watchdog. Without making a sound, he watched me leave, and he probably fell asleep as soon I was gone. Nobody woke up, not even Silva, whom everyone thought could hear a coyote creeping around the house.

When I was half a mile from the hacienda, I looked back one more time. I wasn't able to recognize anything other than the spotlights mounted on the gate and the high enclosure wall.

I didn't have to hurry, but I went on quickly. There were more than four hours until dawn.

A hard wind blew in my face, pulling away my memories of the hacienda as if it didn't want me to remember. I thought of Carmelita, and I knew it would hurt her when she realized I was gone. She was the only one difficult to leave behind. The cold around me started to dig in, but nobody could stop me. I had destroyed my dreams myself.

*

For three days, I watched the captain. I watched him in the morning when he came to the police station. I watched him at noon when he ate at the El Gallo Pinto, a restaurant at the end of the street. He always sat at the same table and on the same chair, with his back to the wall and his face to the street. He drank beer and read the newspaper until they brought his meal. He also read the newspaper while he ate, and when he was done eating he would fold the paper and lay it next to his plate on the table. He would drink a cup of coffee, pay, stand up and walk back to the jail. Most of the people he encountered knew him. They greeted him, and he greeted them, and sometimes they would exchange a few words. Sometimes, with the sleeve of his uniform, he would polish the gold badge on his chest. He laughed with the women and children, and once helped an old lady across the street.

One day, after he had left, I went into the restaurant and took the newspaper from the table. The waitress who had served him saw me.

"What do you want with the paper?" she asked.

"Read it," I answered.

She smiled and let me go.

I sat on a bench in the park and paged through the paper. There was no picture of Don Fernando inside. But I found his name in a headline: "Judge Ochoa's decision strikes a massive blow against the Drug Mafia."

It took me a great while to read the article. The high court had sentenced a man named Miguel Saldivar-Otero to life in prison. He was a drug kingpin with connections to corrupt government officials and police officers.

I read a few other articles, because I had nothing to do

but wait. Somewhere in Europe, where a war was going on, peacekeepers had discovered a mass grave. Hundreds of people had been murdered and buried there. And the negotiations in Chiapas went on. The rebels were prepared to comply with the demands of the government and to lay down their weapons.

A photo showed one of the rebel leaders with a ski cap over his head and face, flanked by other rebels with similar ski caps. I only knew the one in the middle. Through the holes, I could see his light-colored eyes. It was Subcomandante Marcos, the commander of the Zapatista National Liberation Army. I had seen him in our village once with my father. He gave a speech standing on a platform on the plaza behind the soccer goal.

"Today we say, it is enough," he had cried over our heads, and his voice carried to the farthest corners of the village. "Today we say, it is enough. Enough injustice. Enough exploitation. Enough oppression. Enough is enough."

At noon on the fourth day, I went to the restaurant and waited until the captain came out.

It was a lovely afternoon. Smog hung over the city, muting the sunlight. Few people were on the street. No one was nearby. I had hidden the revolver under my shirt, my finger on the trigger. I only stood there and waited. He came directly toward me. At first, he did not know me. Though, something gave him pause. His eyes widened a bit. His step hesitated. Then he stopped, looking at me.

"Santiago Molina," I said. "You remember me, you pig."

"What do you want?" he asked. Sweat suddenly glistened on his forehead.

"Kneel down," I said.

He laughed. "What kind of idiocy…"

"Kneel down, you pig."

He wouldn't kneel down. Not for a kid like me. I took the

revolver from under my shirt, and I shot him in the chest.

He groaned as he dropped to his knees. I shot again, and he looked at me in disbelief. I saw the light flicker in his eyes as he remembered me.

The waitress ran out of the restaurant and screamed for the police. I turned and ran away, and no one tried to stop me because I still held the revolver in my hand and I was ready to shoot anyone.

*

At the bus station in Morelia, I saw a man pick a newspaper out of the trash and read it. When his bus came, he left it behind, half of it on the bench and the other half on the ground. I sat down where he had been and read it. I read about myself as if I were someone else.

BOY KILLS POLICE CHIEF
Motive unknown for the cowardly act

Shortly after he had taken his midday meal in a restaurant not far from the Inner City Police Station, an assassination attempt was carried out on Captain Luis Francisco Figueroa Mendoza.

According to eyewitness reports, a boy about thirteen to fifteen years old waited for the captain on the quiet street and brought him down with two shots from a .38 special revolver. "Everything happened very fast," reported Magdalene Ortiz, a waitress in the restaurant where the captain had eaten shortly before. "The kid said something to him, and the captain laughed. Then the boy pulled a weapon from under his shirt and fired. The captain fell to his knees, and then the kid shot him again. I saw everything through the door. It was horrible.

Everything happened so fast. When I ran out, it was too late. The kid ran down the street with the revolver in his hand. I looked into his eyes as he fled. The eyes of a kid who must have been coughed up by Hell. I think he would have killed anyone who tried to stop him."

Colleagues of Captain Mendoza, who arrived at the scene of the crime only a few minutes later, searched in vain for the "Kid Bandido". There was no sign of him, but the waitress stated that he had attracted her attention the day before when, at about the same time of day, he entered the restaurant and left with a newspaper the captain had been reading at lunch.

Captain Mendoza was a long-time officer in the service of our city police, highly regarded by his colleagues. Nobody knows why this "Kid Bandido" ambushed him. There is no motive and no trace. The captain himself was not yet in a position to comment under the circumstances. After his admittance into the intensive care ward of the hospital, both bullets were removed surgically. The captain's condition is no longer acutely life-threatening.

The police gave out following description of the offender: a young Mexican, probably of Indian background. Medium height. Dark skin. Black, shoulder-length hair parted in the middle. Dark eyes with a greenish cast. Wearing a beige shirt, new blue jeans and brown leader cowboy boots. The suspect is armed.

The police are warning the public not to try to catch this criminal. He is armed and dangerous. Anyone who sees him should exercise the utmost caution and immediately report any information to the nearest police station.

In the paper, there was a photo of the waitress. She had a frightened expression and was pointing, probably in the direction I had run.

I lay the paper on the bench and looked around. It looked like nobody had any interest in me. A bus driver stood on the curb and smoked a cigarette. He did not even look at me as I stood up. I went across the plaza and bought a comb and a pair of scissors in a department store. The sales lady was nice. I told her I wanted to cut my little dog's hair. She looked at me quite strangely, as if I were an angel or something. As she was messing around in the cash register, I stole a small pocket mirror from the shelf and hid it under my shirt.

I went into a public toilet and cut my hair short. Very short. It didn't look bad in the half-light, but outside in the sun, when I looked in the mirror again, I got scared. My scalp shone through everywhere. I looked like a dog with mange. My eyes looked back at me like they belonged to someone who wanted to kill me. I grinned angrily. "Fuck you," I cursed. "Fuck you, you son of a bitch."

I had heard that once in a film. At the theater in Tuxtla Gutiérrez. Before the rebellion, we sometimes went there to the movies. Almost the entire village. Everybody in Pablo Aguirre's truck. Then soldiers killed Pablo on the second day of the rebellion. With a machine gun, as he ran along a roadside ditch with his machete, shouting, "Enough is enough!"

I put away the mirror, pushed the revolver deeper into the waistband of my pants and made my way out of the city. Nobody paid attention to me.

Not even the police driving by in a patrol car. I stopped and laughed and waved at both police officers. One waved back.

I sat down in the grass, and I read the article once again. And I wished I could tell someone the truth. Only I did not know to who. I had no idea which was worse: what he had done to me or what I had done to him. I also did not know whether the two balanced each other out. On God's scale, or on the Devil's. Or on any scale used for weighing rice or corn. All I knew for sure was that there was another truth not printed in the newspaper. I would have liked to shout it out, but nobody would have believed me. Not me.

6
Lucia

I was looking for a place to rest, when I noticed her on the other side of the road. She sat there by the curb in dry grass with her little cat in her lap. She squinted at me because the sun was in her eyes.

I crossed the road looking at her. She had an oddly attractive face in which not much harmonized, yet somehow fit together wonderfully. I had never looked at a more beautiful face, except for my sister Theresa's. Her black hair came just past her shoulders and parted in the middle. Perhaps she was an Indian, but her skin was lighter than mine, and her face was narrow. Her nose was rather small, and, obvious to me, it had been broken at some point.

"What's your name?" I asked her when I got to the other side of the road, standing in front of her.

"Lucia," she said, shading her eyes with her hand. "And yours?"

"Jimmy Molina," I said.

She bent over to stroke her cat and her hair fell, covering her face.

"Jimmy Molina?" she repeated. "Jimmy?"

I grinned. "My name is Santiago."

She nodded as if she already knew that.

"It has no name," she said from behind her hair without raising her head.

"It is only a cat," I said. "I had a dog without a name, until a girl named him Rata."

"Do you want to give it a name?"

"Me?" I laughed.

"What is there to laugh about?"

"That's not something a man would do," I said. "Only girls give names to animals."

"And you're a man?"

"I think so."

"You think that not giving a pet a name makes someone a man?"

"That's not what I said."

She looked at me more closely.

"You are rather thin for a man."

I didn't answer.

"Chico," she said. "I will name my cat Chico."

"Show me." I reached my hand out, but she didn't understand what I wanted from her. She jerked back and her expression hardened. After I explained, she gave me the cat.

"It is a female," I said after I raised its tail briefly.

"The cat is a female?"

"Yes. Don't tell me you don't know how to recognize that."

"Of course I do."

She took back the cat and lifted herself off the wall where she had been sitting.

"I need to go now."

"Where to?"

She turned around and left. At first, I didn't want to let her go, but she just let me stand there, and I watched her, while she climbed over the bricks and pieces of cement, stepped out of the wall's shadow and went down the narrow street leading to the stream, which hadn't been a stream for a long time. She moved lightly on her feet, yet with the caution of a person who was accustomed to danger. I watched her and hoped she would look back once more, but she didn't.

"Stubborn little girl," I muttered.

Then I ran after her and caught up at a street crossing near an old building that had once been a store. I grabbed her by the arm, but she quickly pulled herself free.

"Don't grab me again," she warned me.

"Why not come with me?" I asked her.

"Why should I come with you?"

"Because you probably don't have a home either."

"I have a home."

"Here?"

"No. Back there, where I come from."

"Where do you come from?"

"From San Javier."

"Where is that?"

"Back there, where my family lives."

"And where is that?"

"In Guatemala."

"Did you flee from there?"

"Yes."

"Alone?"

"No. With a boy and my mother."

"Where are they?"

She shrugged her shoulders.

"You do not know where they are?"

"No. They left our camp and went back because now there is supposed to be peace in Guatemala."

"There will never be peace as long as any of us are alive."

"This could be."

"Come with me."

She cocked her head and looked into my eyes.

"You are alone, right?" I said.

She was silent.

"If you come with me, you will not be alone anymore."

"I like being alone."

"I don't believe you."

"I like being alone."

"I am going to America," I said.

"I have already met a few on this road who want to go there," she said.

"Where are you going?"

"I am going there, too."

"Alone?"

"Yes."

"Why not go with me?"

"I don't think it would be good, Jimmy Molina," she said.

"And can you tell me why?"

"Because I am a girl and you are a boy."

I grinned.

She nodded. "Look at you," she said. "I don't like the way you look at me when you grin."

"Why not?"

"Because I know what you are thinking."

"And what am I thinking?"

"What all guys think."

"You're wrong. I'm looking at you thinking you are a very beautiful girl."

She looked at the ground trying to escape me.

"Who broke your nose?"

She raised her head. The light in her eyes turned hard. "And the scars on your chin and your wrist?"

"I don't think it is of your concern."

"Do you know what else I think? I think you are rather complicated for your age."

"And you are rather bold in the way you look at me."

I wanted to take her arm again, but she moved back, and the cat snarled at me.

We went down the street together, the sun in our faces. Below, in the valley, shadows of the houses in a small village lay in an odd haze of light and dust, in which the asphalt of the main road shone. In the distance, cars and people seemed to move about soundlessly.

"What are you running from?" I asked her.

"From nothing."

"I have never before met a girl who was on her way to America completely alone."

"I'm not alone."

"You are not alone?" I looked around quickly, but I could not see anyone who might be with her. Then she laughed.

"You are with me."

"Me? Tell me, are you maybe crazy? We have only just now met."

"But I know who you are."

"You know who I am?"

"Yes."

"And where do you know that from?"

"The cat told me who you are."

"The cat?"

"Yes, the cat."

"And what did the cat tell you about me?"

"That you are Santiago Molina, and you are running from the police because a few days ago you shot down a police captain."

Shocked, I stopped walking and grabbed her by the arm. "You read that in the newspaper," I struck back. "The cat certainly cannot read."

"You are a dangerous pistolero, Jimmy Molina!"

"That is true," I said with defiance. "What else is bugging you?"

"You had better let go of me," she said, and her voice shook.

"And if I don't?"

She struck out with her free hand and hit me so suddenly I wasn't able to get out of the way. I let her go. My cheek burned like fire.

"I warned you," I heard her say. "I don't want to have anything to do with you, understand? I don't want to go to

America with you. I do not want to be seen with you, and I also don't want to hitch rides with you. Do you understand, Jimmy Molina?"

I looked at her angrily.

"I could kill you," I said.

"The way you shoth down the captain?"

"What else should I have done? The captain was the law. Where could I have gone to get him punished for what he'd done? Who would have prevented him from doing it to others again and again?"

She turned around and went away.

*

The next evening, I saw her sitting under a tree. She was eating a piece of papaya. Dust sticking to her skin and covering her legs, and the dress she wore was dirty and torn. She had a blood-crusted scrape on her left ankle. When she saw me, she furrowed her brow and threatened me with a flash from her black eyes.

"Keep on going," she said before I was ten steps away from her.

I went by her without saying anything and without looking at her.

"Hey."

I stopped.

"Do you want a piece of papaya?"

"Are you speaking to me, perhaps?"

"Who else? There's nobody else traveling on this road."

"How is it that you're on this road? It's not the main road."

She pushed strands of hair out of her face.

"Have you been following me?" I asked.

"No."

"You lie."

"I never lie."

"You lie."

I went over to her in the shade. The little cat lay sleeping in her lap.

"How's Chico?"

"Good."

"Has she perhaps read today's newspaper?"

"There is nothing about you in it today."

"Then they have already forgotten."

"Hardly. It says in the article that the captain will live, but he will be paralyzed for the rest of his life and no longer able to do his work."

I lay back, folded my hands behind my head and looked up at the crown of the tree, a tangle of branches and leaves through which I could see flecks of the sky.

"It also says they are searching for you everywhere, and they will not stop until they have found you."

"They will have to search for a long time, then."

"Someone could betray you."

"You?"

"No. But someone who knows about you."

"Nobody knows about me."

"People you have come in contact with."

I thought of the haciendero and his family. He must have read the reports in the newspaper. He was an intelligent man, and by now somebody, possibly Pedro, may have discovered the revolver was missing.

"Would you like to tell me why you shot down the captain?" she asked.

"I told you already."

She said nothing. If she had asked me whether I did it for revenge, I probably would have admitted it to her. Maybe she didn't ask because she knew it anyway.

"Yesterday your dress was completely in order. Why is it so dirty and torn?"

"Yesterday I told you what men think when they see me." She leaned toward me. "Here. This papaya is sweet as sugar."

I slowly sat down. She offered me a piece of papaya she had cut with a knife. I took it from her hand and began to eat. At the same time, I started to think about what men think when they see Lucia. I thought about how I wanted to touch her with my hands. I wanted to feel her smooth, dusty skin and her hair and her eyes that were a different shape and her small nose, and her chin and her throat and her body and her legs and I thought it would be more beautiful than a dream to make love to her. At the same time, though, it made no sense to think about it, for I was not a person powerful enough to make his dreams come true. Only Don Fernando thought so, but I was not.

*

We lay down under the tree, and the stars glittered through the tangle of branches and leaves.

"We should leave," she said after we had not said a word to each other for almost an hour.

I lay still.

"It's cool now," she said. "We should leave and keep going."

"I thought you didn't want to be seen with me."

"It's night. Nobody will see us."

We got up, pulled our stuff together and went out into the night, walking on our shadows, the moon directly above us. We walked northward next to each other on the old country road. We heard dogs barking, and we saw lights and the outlines of houses that stood alone. We went through a sleeping village and through another village, where music came out of a cantina. Then we crossed a dry streambed and the road we were following connected to an asphalt road upon which trucks drove by to the north and south.

"How come you found me?" she suddenly asked me. We were walking one behind the other on a narrow path below the embankment. The path had been trampled by horses and donkeys and cows and led through the underbrush yet it always followed the road.

"I saw how you climbed into the back of a small truck. Then the truck turned off the main road."

"There were two men," she said. "And a large dog."

"What did they do to you?"

"Nothing. I ran away."

"And the dog?"

"They wanted the dog to chase after me, but the dog would not obey them. I heard them cursing, and then they hit the dog, but the dog still did not obey them. Then they ran after me, but after a while, they gave up because they could see they would never catch me."

"And the papaya?"

"What about it?"

"Where did you get the papaya?"

"They had melons and papayas in the back of the truck. I took the papaya when I ran away."

"You stole the papaya?"

"That is not as bad as shooting a police captain."

"It depends on—"

"On what?"

I stopped talking. After a while, I said, "We could try to hitchhike for a bit."

"Nobody would pick us up. Not the both of us and not in the middle of the night. The chances of someone not seeing us on the side of the road and running us over with his truck are better than someone stopping and taking us along."

"If you stand alone by the side of the road, there is a good chance someone will stop."

"And you?"

"I will hide in the brush."

"But how could I trust you, with that revolver stuck under your waistband?"

"You can trust me."

She stopped walking.

"Never," she said.

*

The truck stopped at a rest area. Its motor was running, but the headlights were off, only the small parking lights were glowing.

The driver stood at the edge of the parking area, pissing into the bushes. As he finished, Lucia stepped out from the shadow of an acacia. He first saw her as he was buttoning up his pants. A single lamp glowed at the far end of the parking lot. Another truck was there in the dark, and its motor was not running. At the other end of the rest area a motorhome with an American license plate was parked.

"Hi," Lucia said.

"Hi," said the truck driver looking Lucia over from head to foot.

"Can you take me with you?" she asked.

"Where to?"

"To Nogales."

"Nogales? I am not going to Nogales." He wanted to go to his truck, but Lucia stepped into his path.

"Where are you going?" she asked him.

"To Hermosillo."

"How far is it from there to the border?"

"Not far. Listen, girl, I have a job to do and no interest in taking you along." He pushed her aside and circled his truck, checking all the wheels. When he came around to the driver's compartment again, Lucia was standing on the running board. "You are driving alone through the night," she said. "If you take me along, I will talk with you. That way you will not fall asleep."

He looked at her once again.

"How old are you?"

"Eighteen."

He shook his head. "You are no more than fourteen. I have a daughter your age. I know all about it."

"I have a newspaper I could read to you," she said.

He laughed. "Are you alone?"

She dropped her head, and he immediately knew what was happening. He knew she could not lie to him, because she had a functioning conscience.

"You are not alone, right?"

"Yes."

He looked around, and then I stepped out from behind the truck with the .38 in my hand. He breathed in sharply.

"Climb in," I said.

He seemed to understand people. He knew right away that, in contrast to Lucia's, my conscience no longer functioned properly.

"He will not do anything to you if you take us along," said Lucia. She opened the driver's door and climbed in first. She slid to the far end of the seat and cranked down the side window.

"Climb in," I ordered the truck driver.

"Think about it, kid. I have a family."

"You talk too much."

He grabbed a handgrip on the truck, swung himself onto the running board and climbed in. As he sat down behind the steering wheel, I got around the truck and climbed in on the other side. Lucia slid to the middle.

"Thank you for taking us along," she said to him. "We have come almost a hundred kilometers on foot."

He nodded. "It is over seven hundred kilometers to Hermosillo. Too far to walk."

"The sooner you start driving, the faster we will get there," I said and pulled the plug on the microphone of the CB-radio under the dashboard.

He looked at me. I still had the revolver in my hand. He turned on the headlights, put the truck in first gear and released the handbrake. The giant truck shuddered as it started to move.

"What's your load?" Lucia asked him.

"Nuts and bolts," he said. "For the Ford plant in Hermosillo."

The truck slowly picked up speed. After we had traveled a bit, I stuck the revolver into the waistband of my pants in a way that wouldn't bother me while I was sitting. I opened my shirt so I would be able to grab it quickly at any time. Then I made myself as comfortable as possible and closed my eyes.

"My name is Ramon," I heard the truck driver say. "Ramon Fuentes."

"I'm Lucia."

"And him?"

"His name is Jimmy," she answered. "My cat is called Chico, even though it's a girl."

I was already almost asleep, but I still heard him begin to talk about his family, about his wife and his children, and about a pregnant bitch named Luna who had one brown eye and one blue.

*

I woke up when the truck began to slow down. At first, I didn't know where I was. Then I reached for the revolver, but it was no longer in my pants.

"The pistol slid out of your pants while you were asleep," the driver said without taking his eyes off the exit ramp to a filling station. I sat up. Lucia lay huddled next to me, her legs pulled up close to her body and her head on my left thigh. She had folded one arm behind the back of her neck and the other hung at her side down onto the floorboard.

"Here." He held the revolver out to me, grip first. "Is this the pistol you used to gun down the police captain?"

"It's not a pistol," I said, even though in Mexico everyone says "pistol" whether it is a revolver or not. "Una pistola" was a handgun.

I pushed Lucia's head off my thigh and rose up enough to free my right arm, which was wedged between the bench and the door.

Lucia awoke startled.

"Where are we?" she asked. She rubbed her eyes as she stared through the windshield at the filling station.

"North of Durango," said the truck driver. "There are still a bit more than five hundred kilometers to Hermosillo."

"Why are we stopping here?"

"Because I need diesel."

"Diesel?"

"Gasoline."

He drove the truck up to one of the pumps and stopped without turning off the engine.

"I have to go in there, kid," he said and motioned with his head at a store, over which a neon sign for Tecate beer blinked on and off. Two men stood at the entrance. One was smoking. The other talked, gesticulating at the same time with both hands.

"Let's go," I said to him.

We climbed out. All three of us. Lucia held the cat in her arms. In the store, the truck driver talked with a man who had come out of the shop rubbing his oil-smeared hands with a rag. He stood next to a shelf with newspapers.

"Do they belong to you?" the man asked the driver.

"I am taking them along as far as Hermosillo," said the truck driver. "They are brother and sister who are on their way home."

The man looked a Lucia. She stroked her cat.

The man bared his teeth and it confused me. He bared his teeth and looked at her quite oddly.

"If you both want to stay here overnight, I have room for you and your cute sister," he said.

"They do not want to stay here, you old geezer," the truck driver said, laughing. "Go and fill up the tanks. Then your thoughts will be on something else."

The man also laughed and went out.

"Thanks," Lucia muttered.

"What for?"

"That you said that."

"Forget it," said Ramon. He pulled three Cokes out of the cooler and gave both of us our own bottle.

"Earlier, when I was a kid, I went to America, too," he said as he lifted the Coke bottle in a toast to that nation. "I was my father's oldest son, and my father was the oldest son of his father. The eldest son always goes to America and earns money to send home. It has been this way with us ever since there was a border between our two countries."

"Is this border the only thing separating us?" I said.

He smiled. "Yes, I do believe so. The Americans could be Mexicans, and the Mexicans could be Americans. Maybe, one of these days, there will be no border, and we'll be one big nation."

"How was it in America?" Lucia asked him.

"I thought it would rain gold there," he said and drank his Coke.

"It didn't rain gold?" Lucia acted surprised.

"Around Houston, I got caught in a terrible storm, and almost drowned," he said. "I was standing in a dried-out bed of a stream, and suddenly, all that water came. I just stood there and waited for the gold, but it didn't come."

"Maybe it's different now than it was before," I said.

He looked at me. "Not likely. There are storms, but there are always people who give you shelter, kid. That is how gringos are. Very few bad ones, but most of them are helpful when you're in dire straights. I don't remember a single bad thing happening to me when I was a boy in the United States of America."

Lucia smiled. "I'm going to Hollywood," she said. "There, it does rain gold."

He bowed his head. "May it rain gold for you, Lucia," he said without looking up at her.

Afterward, we were silent. I took a magazine from the rack and leafed through it without looking at the pictures or reading anything. Lucia sat on a stool by the cash register and played with the cat in her lap. The cat bit her on the finger without hurting her. Then the owner of the filling station came in and wrote the bill, and the truck driver signed it.

"Are you sure you don't want to stay here, girl?" the man asked.

We left and traveled on.

*

The police had set up a roadblock. If I hadn't turned off the CB radio, perhaps we might have been warned. So we first noticed the roadblock as we were coming around a long, drawn-out curve and saw the lights on the road and the two spotlights glaring up the sides.

"Damned cops," roared the truck driver. "For sure, Raoul back at the filling station recognized you, kid. If I was able to recognize you."

I pulled the revolver out from under my shirt, pushed Lucia back in the seat hard with my elbow, leaned over toward him and put the barrel to his temple.

"Stop this truck."

"It is too late, kid. I can—"

"Stop, dammit!" I screamed. It was no more than three or four hundred meters to the roadblock and the road sloped slightly, but Ramon hit the brakes immediately. The truck, carrying a heavy load, seemed about to jackknife. I heard the brakes hiss and the tires squeal, and I saw Lucia stretch out both hands to support herself on the dashboard. At that moment, the truck broke sharply to the left. I lost my balance and got thrown against the door. I heard Lucia scream, and I saw Ramon counter steer. His face distorted to a grimace; he seemed to be screaming, but no sound came from his mouth. Our headlights shone across a guard rail and out into the landscape. The truck, squeaking and groaning, made a couple of side hops. Lucia's hand was suddenly on my face. The windshield shattered. The side door popped open, and I saw the spotlights and the police, who were jumping aside in the blinding light as if trying to dodge a monster. The truck spun and crashed into the guardrail, slid along it to the first spotlight and hit one of the police cars on the side of the road. A siren howled. The truck's motor stopped and we hit the guardrail a second time, sliding along it until we finally stopped in a cloud of dust.

I grabbed Lucia by the arm.

"Out!" I screamed.

She only stared at me. Blood from a scrape on her forehead ran across her face.

I wanted to pull her out with me, but, when I was halfway out of the truck, trying to jump on the running board, I saw that she was resisting, with a foot on the door frame; she was also holding tight to the seat with one hand.

"Come on!" I shouted at her. "Come on, Lucia!"

She did not say a word. She just stared at me with big, shocked eyes. At that moment, I understood that she did not want to come with me. I let go of her, turned around and ran. I jumped over the guardrail and ran down a slope and through the thorn bushes. Voices and flashlights chased after me.

"There he goes!" I heard them shout. "There that bastard goes!"

I didn't pay attention to them. I ran out into the night, and I ran until my lungs burned and my legs could no longer carry me. I stumbled down an embankment into a dry streambed and fell. I fell so hard it knocked the breath out of me. I raised myself out of the sand to get air, and I thought I would suffocate. I thought my head was going to burst. I wanted to scream, but no sound would come out. Wheezing, I sucked the air through my mouth into my lungs, where a fire had started. I rolled onto my back. The stars glowed red over me. My heart raced, and I heard their voices. They came closer. I heard them curse, and then I saw the light from their flashlights through the brush along the bank.

I was able to stand up. I ran across the streambed and crawled under a barbed wire fence, and I ran out to an area where sparse bushes were growing. I ran until I fell into a ditch. I crawled along the ditch and waited for them to find me. They did not come through the streambed. I heard them talking and cursing, but their voices became fainter and fainter. Finally, I did not hear them anymore.

Later, I crawled out of the ditch.

In the distance, I saw the lights of cars and trucks traveling on the road. Very softly, I heard the rumble of motors. I was three or four kilometers away from the road. Alone.

A few feet away, a bony old cow stood with its calf. Both of them watched me trying to get up. When I rose to my feet, the calf trotted away. The cow turned around and followed the calf.

7
Flaco

I took an overland bus to Hermosillo. From there, a man who delivered chicken to Nogales let me ride with him. He had a pickup truck, an old Dodge he had painted mustard-yellow himself. "Pollo Rapido" was written on the side doors. In back, he'd built a cage.

There were at least seven hundred chickens inside. They were so thickly packed together that some of them had pecked the eyes out of their neighbors in panic. A few, lying under the rest, were already dead. Their heads hung from their long necks through the wire mesh of the cage. Others were barely alive; they lay in the cage with beaks wide open, struggling for air.

"They are destined for the restaurants in Nogales," the man explained to me. "The ones dying on the trip won't need to be slaughtered."

Feathers flew behind the pickup in the back draft. The truck's old motor rumbled as if it were running on only six of its eight cylinders. The man said the motor was a reliable one. In almost twenty years, it had never let him down. The man did not have a wife or children. "With women, you only get strife, boy. I don't need anyone to scream at me at home, to keep a sharp eye on me, to tell me what to do or what I've done wrong. Every week, I travel with a load of hens to Nogales. When I get horny, I go to a whorehouse. It costs me a few pesos, but I consider it an investment in my personal freedom."

He talked a whole bunch of stuff that didn't interest me, because his life didn't affect mine. He was driving to Nogales with his half-dead chickens, and next to him, he had a seat free. That was all. I wished he would have closed his mouth and left me to my thoughts, where I was with Lucia and her cat. I had never taken a separation to heart like this one. I didn't know anything about her except that she wanted to go to America. All the same, it seemed we had not met just a few days before, but long ago, in a different time and a different world. Somewhere we had been close, so close I could still sense her now, the movement of her naked skin on mine and her breath on my lips before we kissed. But we had never kissed. I was awake, but I dreamt while the chicken dealer next to me spoke as if he'd discovered the world on his trips from Hermosillo to Nogales. He got on my nerves, and I thought about sticking the barrel of my revolver in his mouth and pulling the trigger, but I didn't want more troubles than I already had. So I let him talk without listening to him. Finally, I told him to stop and let me out. He stopped, and I climbed out as he stared at me in disbelieve.

"There are still more than thirty kilometers to Nogales," he said.

"That's all right."

"Now, watch out for the Federales at the control station. Short ways before you get to Nogales they're hidden in the shrubs lining the road. If they catch you alone, they'll play their games with you."

"What games?"

"They prefer to play their games with gringos, but if they catch you alone, and there is no gringo right there, they will certainly take a fondness for you."

He drove away, stopped again after fifty meters, put the truck in reverse and came rolling back. He leaned out the window, one hand on the steering wheel and scratched his neck with the other.

"If you want to find accommodations in Nogales, pay a visit to old Sarita."

"Who is she?"

"Tell her I sent you."

"And where do I find her?"

"At the Hotel Camino Real. She works there. She procures the coyotes for those who want to cross the border. The old slut's been around the block a few times. And nobody knows her way around this border city better than she does. With her, you find everything you're looking for."

"I am not looking for anything."

"I see in your eyes that you're looking for something. They're keen eyes. Sarita will like you."

He laughed and shifted into first gear. The transmission groaned, and the pickup jerked forward. The dead chicken heads swung from the rusty wire mesh on their long, featherless necks.

"Pollo Rapido" drove away while I stood at the edge of the road. I caught one of the feathers in flight with my hand. I was happy I had not silenced him. I would certainly encounter Lucia again one day, and she certainly would not approve of me shooting him because he talked too much.

*

I arrived in Nogales, Sonora in the evening, not knowing anyone in this border town, feeling lost and longing for Lucia to arrive, so we could leave Mexico together. Hungry and tired, I was looking for a safe place to sleep and something to eat when I saw the boy lying in a ditch in his own blood.

The people standing around him said he had been a "Bajador," one who took shelter in the waste-water canals under the city and wreaked havoc everywhere.

A pregnant girl who was bleeding from her forehead told the police tearfully that the boy's name was Tomo and that he belonged to Flaco's gang, a gang calling itself Barrio Libre Sur.

"He's my husband," the girl cried. "I'm carrying his child."

"He was a dangerous rat," said a man close to me. He said it so loud the girl heard. She turned around, and before the police could stop her, she spat in the man's face.

Nobody knew who had shot Tomo. One of the policemen, a special unit officer with Grupo Beta, said that Tomo also had at least twenty stab wounds. Tomo lay in a canal that was as wide as a paved streambed along a busy road that led to the city center from the south. Cars drove by slowly. Their headlights touched us, brushed across the cracked asphalt and over the walls of half-collapsed old houses where nobody lived, across posters advertising women's underwear and beer. I stood in the crowd, and nobody recognized me.

"Who are the bajadores?" I asked a man nearby.

"Tunnel Kids," he said. "Children living in the canals and tunnels like rats. They should be smoked out or poisoned, but the police won't finish them off." He tried to figure me out. "You're not from here, right?"

"No," I said. "I'm from Chiapas."

"Most of them come here from somewhere else," he said. "They're drifters. They have no families and no homes. They're like vermin. A person could feel pity when seeing that—this pregnant girl and boy lying in his blood—but that would be false. These children are beasts running wild. A public menace. They must be stamped out."

He seemed serious. I left him standing there, and I was thinking I would probably kill him if I met him again somewhere alone.

One of the police officers shined a flashlight in my face.

"Hey, you," he shouted at me.

I ran away, and nobody tried to catch me.

*

I approached a kid hunkering at the edge of the street looking at his basketball shoes and asked him for the way to the Hotel Camino Real.

The kid looked up but didn't answer.

"Do you know which hotel I mean?" I asked.

"Yes, I know."

"Where is it?"

"There." He pointed down the street.

I crossed the intersection and walked along the boardwalk. People passing by didn't pay attention to me, mistaking me for a harmless boy. I stopped in front of the hotel. A yellow neon sign hung over the entrance. In bright red letters it said, "Camino Real," the King's Way. This was the way from Mexico City to Nogales—the path I had taken, and many more before me, none of them a king or a queen.

Across the street from the hotel, I sat down on a bucket and observed the ugly square building. People disappeared into it. People like shadows. Vague shadows among the real people. Noiseless. Quick.

They disappeared through the door of the hotel and did not reappear.

Long after midnight, I was still sitting on the bucket. Then I walked up the street until I came close to the brightly lit border crossing. A building bridged the street. A few cars stood in the glaring light, waiting to be driven slowly through, under the building, across to the other side of the border. They moved as noiseless as the shadows that had disappeared into the Hotel Camino Real.

Here, where I stood, it was still Mexico. There, on the other side of the check point, was the country called the United States of America. I watched the vehicles cross the border.

While it got later, there were fewer and fewer. Then, after midnight there were no more. No cars and no trucks. It was quiet in the city except for dogs barking.

I went back to the hotel and watched the entrance. Shadows no longer entered or left the hotel. The lights at the front door went out. I sneaked to the backyard. There were small shacks and a path between them that led to a side street. I followed it. It ended close to the border. An insurmountable wall of overlapping metal plates loomed over the crest of a steep hill. Above me, on the slope, small houses clung to the face of the hill, digging their claws into the slope with the last of their strength, until one day, too weak, they would lose their grip, slide down in an avalanche into the depths.

I went back to the Hotel Camino Real. A man came out, stopped on the street and lit a cigarette. The flame illuminated his face for a moment. It was the face of a man nervously looking in all directions, a dark face with a mustache. Not an unusual face, but I memorized it and would have known it again among a hundred other average faces.

I waited until he climbed into his car and drove away. I smelled the exhaust in the fresh night air as I crossed the street and approached the hotel entrance. Finally, I decided to enter and ask for Sarita. I broke into a sweat. I sensed quite clearly that it was sweat of fear. I grasped the revolver under my shirt in my waistband, stopped in front of the door and tried breathing deeply to quiet my heart. I tried to think of Lucia, but I was not able to. My thoughts were no longer thoughts. My thoughts were fantasies about what played out behind this door. I grasped the brass knob, turned it and opened the door.

A strange sweetish odor I had never smelled before struck my nose. A lamp hanging from the ceiling by its cord lit a narrow hallway. Its pink light illuminated the hallway and part of the stairway leading up to the second floor. It was dark at the end of the hall, but I heard soft voices from there.

I closed the door behind me. A vase with plastic flowers stood on a desk next to the entrance. The plastic flowers reeked like the air. Only much stronger. It was an odor that made me feel dopey and revolted me. A few keys hung on a key rack. A swivel chair with torn upholstery stood by a vending machine. On the wall hung a calendar with a picture of a Spanish matador in battle with a bull, his sword raised for the death blow.

I hit the bell on the desk.

The voices at the end of the hall fell silent. I waited. Nothing happened. Once again, I rang the bell.

A door opened and closed somewhere.

A man came out from behind the stairs. He was a small, wiry man who bore similarities to a rodent. I did not like him.

"What do you want?" he asked.

"Someone sent me to Sarita," I said. My mouth was dry and my voice sounded hoarse.

"What do you want from her?"

"I will tell her that when I see her."

He examined me. Then he went back to where he came from without saying a word. I waited. I waited for at least three or four minutes. Then Sarita appeared. She was a tall slender woman in a black dress with long sleeves buttoned up to her neck. Her dark hair was combed straight back and tied in a knot. She didn't just look at me. Her eyes searched for an opening through which she could invade me. I gave nothing away. I just stood there and coldly met her gaze, my hand on the grip of the gun. My finger was bent, touching the trigger.

"Who are you?" she asked.

"Santiago," I said.

"And who sent you?"

"No one. A chicken merchant told me your name, Señora."

"This could have been only one person," she said. "A foolish man."

"A talkative man," I said.

She almost smiled.

"Where do you come from, Santiago?"

"From Chiapas."

"And where do you want to go?"

"Nowhere."

"Nowhere?"

"No, I am staying here."

She tilted her head to one side. At one time, she might have been a beautiful woman. I did not know how old she was and what life had done to her, but her face was spotted and almost transparent, and there was an emptiness in her eyes.

"You can't stay here with me," she said.

"Why not?"

"Because nobody stays here. People come and go."

"Where should I go?"

"Go to Flaco."

There it was again. That name.

"Somebody killed Tomo," I said.

"What do you know about it?"

"Nothing. By chance, I was passing by when they found him."

She nodded as if I had told her something about myself or Tomo she had long known.

"If you want to stay here, go to Flaco," she said once again.

"And where do I find him?"

"With the kids in the tunnels. Flaco is a bajador."

"They say there are many tunnels," I said. "And many bajadores."

"There are two main tunnels," she explained. "One of them

begins at the end of the street. Ask for Flaco, the King of this tunnel. Everyone knows him."

"Who says I want to meet him?"

"You," she said matter-of-factly. "You do not want to go anywhere, Santiago." Now she smiled, although it didn't quite look like a smile. One corner of her mouth changed and that changed her face also, but not her dark eyes. "Someone who does not want to go anywhere has arrived."

She turned around and left. I watched her until she disappeared behind the stairway. Then the little man appeared again.

"Get lost, punk," he said.

He had no idea how close to death he was. I had to force my hand not to draw the gun from my waistband. In the light of the lamp, I saw his prominent teeth. He wore a T-shirt, blue jeans and basketball shoes. I memorized his face. His face was also not unusual. I had seen it all over Mexico on men I had encountered fleetingly on any street in any city. Flat, with broad cheekbones and slanted eyes. Nonetheless, I would never forget this man's face.

I turned around and left, the cold rage eroding me. I tried to think of Lucia, but I only thought about killing the man. After a while, I stopped and rubbed my face to try to get my mind to focus on other things.

I was ready to annihilate the world. I could have killed everyone. Except for Lucia. For a moment, I was almost afraid of myself. I tried to determine whether I was at the point of killing myself.

*

I stood in a ditch that began at the opening of a square tunnel and ran about a hundred meters along the foot of a hill before it turned into a broader canal where there was a massive steel grating, upon which hung all sorts of garbage driven down by flooding. The concrete slabs of the tunnel projected out of the steep embankment. In the distance, I could see the hill over which ran the metal wall, separating the United States of America from Mexico.

The large concrete canal was about twenty feet wide and led into a square tunnel over which a road crossed with wire fence running on both sides. Floodwater had taken pieces of concrete from the foundation at the end of the tunnel, creating a large gap between the tunnel and the canal. From this gap a footpath led through flood plain overgrown with high grass to the rear entrance of the Hotel Camino Real. I followed this path in the moonlight, climbed through a fence and into the canal and got to the bottom in front of the tunnel's entrance.

I picked up a board in a pile of rubble and placed it slanting against the edge of the tunnel's foundation, which was about three feet above me. I used the board as a bridge to get into the tunnel. Supporting myself with one hand on the wall of the tunnel, at first, I stood slightly bent over and listened into the darkness. From the depth of the tunnel came a strange noise that sounded like a muffled, swelling rush. It was like hearing ocean surf far in the distance. I also sensed a cold draft that stank of feces and urine. There I stood, at the entrance to an underworld. I knew nothing more than the name Flaco. I had arrived at the end of my journey, which had begun in a small village in Chiapas when I was born. Was I really where I wanted to be as the woman in the hotel had said? Or had I woken from an ugly dream to seek shelter in a nightmare?

I looked back over the broad cement ditch, pale and dry in the moonlight. I could have gone back to the hotel. I could have crept into the city somewhere to wait for dawn. But the urge to go into the tunnel was stronger than the fear digging its claws into me.

Bent over, with my head drawn back, I moved into the darkness. After a few steps, I stopped and looked back. A streetlight far away glowed like the round eye of a night owl watching me.

I went farther, one hand on the wall, counting my steps. My feet came up against all sorts of things I couldn't identify. Garbage had collected in piles with branches from shrubs and trees, rags and shredded plastic bags, glass shards, paper and other worthless stuff, even to someone who owned nothing.

I had taken sixty-one steps when I suddenly heard voices behind me. They came from the entrance of the tunnel. It sounded like two men in conversation, but I couldn't understand their words. I crouched down and made myself as small as possible. The beam of a flashlight moved along the concrete walls with ghostly silence. The light touched me briefly, gliding over me and passing through the black depth that seemed to have no end. For seconds, the area near me was brightly lit. The light crept along, lighting the walls like the pale stretched belly of a dead snake. I waited for a sound of surprise, but whoever was shining the light didn't see me.

Then the flashlight switched off, and I got up quickly and went on. From nervousness, I forgot to count my steps.

For a long while, it remained quiet behind me. Then I encountered new noises. Whispering voices of men, women and children. I hurried on until I spotted a weak light in front of me. Steely cold light came from a narrow cement shaft leading upward. Iron rungs embedded in the shaft led about four meters up to a rectangular drain cover. The light of a street lamp seeped through a half dozen narrow openings in the drain cover. Without thinking twice, I reached for the rungs, pulled myself up and climbed to the drain cover. When

I pushed against it with one shoulder, it yielded with a loud shriek. Using a little strength, I was able to push it away. I lifted it to one side and carefully, avoiding loud noise, let it down next to the opening.

Under me, the beam of a flashlight darted through the tunnel.

I climbed through and into the open. I found myself at a deserted intersection, standing under a streetlight that brightly illuminated the entire crossing. The houses looming up around me were dark. DON'T WALK shone at me from a traffic light. A giant billboard burned the redness of a Coca-Cola advertisement, and in a gap between the houses stood cars with American license plates behind a wire fence.

Suddenly, I realized I was on the other side of the border. In the United States of America.

I grabbed the drain cover, raised it up and tried to lay it lightly over the drainage shaft. I was not successful. A loud, metallic ringing cut through the stillness of the night as I let go of it. It fell into its sunken iron frame. When the noise from the drain cover died out, no more voices came from below. The tunnel down there was dark and without life, but I knew it was only an illusion. Eyes glowed. Hearts pounded. Blood rushed through the arteries of people who, at that moment, were standing still and holding their breath, because they'd suddenly become aware of the danger still threatening while they took their last steps toward freedom.

*

I lay on the cold asphalt, so close to the curb that someone happening by scarcely would have noticed me. The drain cover was directly in front of my face. With one eye, I stared through the slits in the opening down to the tunnel, about four meters under me. For a few minutes, it was completely dark down there. I picked up the same unusual rushing noise from before. I lay still, but I was ready to pull my head back quickly if someone appeared below.

Gradually, my eyes got used to the dim light falling through the slits of the drain cover into the shaft. In this light, which was slightly more than a glimmer, a shadowy figure suddenly appeared directly below me. It persisted for a few seconds, motioned with one hand into the dark, and before it occurred to me to pull back my head, it had disappeared again.

Then, others followed, closely packed, one after another. I heard their gasping breath and their quick steps on the cement. I listened to a woman's voice whisper something and a man answered her. I saw outstretched hands seeking other hands or pressing the wall of the tunnel as they went along. I saw the face of someone who looked up, surprised by the light falling through the drain cover. "America," someone called softly. "Is this America up there?"

The shadows flitting by came to a stop. Some remained directly below me, so close together I could see the glimmer of several faces with hopeful yet fearful eyes lit by an American streetlamp.

"Is someone up there?" an anxious voice asked, followed by shriek from a child.

"I'm one of you," I quickly answered. "Is Lucia with you?"

"A girl with her cat?"

"Quiet!" ordered another voice. "Move on! Go on! Go on, dammit!"

The shadows pushed on, and when the last one had passed by me, I stood up. I had no idea where I should go, so I went along the street leading in the same direction as the tunnel.

*

They came out of a drainage ditch under a narrow bridge like sheep being driven by dogs. They stepped out from under the shadow of the bridge with garbage bags, and sacks of canvas and purses and small suitcases. Women and men pulled children along with them. A girl holding a baby in one arm tried at the same time to carry an overly stuffed suitcase hanging from a strap over her shoulder. The strap fell and made her hesitate as she ran, but the people behind her pushed her on. She almost tripped, but a boy grabbed her by the arm and pulled her along, and she slid the case behind her on the asphalt.

The man who was the first out of the ditch indicated the way with an outstretched hand toward a dark street where two pickup trucks sat with their motors running. One had a tarp cover; the other carried a camper. The door of the camper stood wide open. A man jumped out and ran to the rear of the other pickup and opened the tarp by quickly pulling the bungee cords. With a small flashlight, he helped the people run across the street from the bridge.

"Over here!" he called to them. "West coast in the truck! East coast in the camper! Move your asses!"

The people divided into two groups. The girl with the child hurried to the camper. One of the men helped them climb onto the rear bumper. I saw the girl's face briefly with the flashlight. She turned around at the last moment before she disappeared into the camper, as if saying goodbye to someone or something. Dark hair hung down her forehead. She was beautiful, perhaps sixteen or seventeen years old. I didn't know why, but she reminded me of my sister Theresa. I hadn't thought about Theresa in a long time. But I remembered her as I had seen her last, running out of our house with her bundle and turning her head once more before climbing into the truck with Pablo.

I was about to leave my hiding place and run across the street when I spotted a car without its lights on rolling between the houses, moving almost noiselessly to the two pickup trucks. It was a green off-road vehicle, a Chevy Blazer, and I immediately saw the sign on the driver's door. It looked like the sign on a Federales police car. But this was not Mexico, and the Blazer was no police car.

I stopped as if lightning had struck me. I wanted to shout out a warning. "La Migra," it yelled inside me without sound. The next moment, the man standing in the middle of the street noticed the car. His warning shout was drowned out by the roaring of an engine. On the other side of the street, where a few corrugated-metal sheds stood, two vehicles shot out, tires squealing over the potholed asphalt, and stopped crossways in front of both trucks. Even before the vehicles came to a stop, spotlights went on. Glaring light flooded the place.

I saw the man on the street run away. He ran onto the bridge to the other side of the ditch. Uniformed border patrol officers jumped out of their cars, their weapons ready to shoot, and took cover behind their car doors. A voice from a loudspeaker ordered in Spanish, "Stop! Stay where you are! Nobody move!" Women and children screamed. A gunshot ripped through the night. The man who ran across the bridge and into the ditch shot at the patrol cars, but he missed them and hit one of the metal sheds. The officers shot back, one with a shotgun. The man, who was almost at the end of the bridge, suddenly fell as if pushed hard from behind. He fell to his knees and immediately got up again, but he could no longer keep his balance, and he staggered around as if drunk. They shot him again and brought him down just as it appeared he would make it into the ditch. I looked over to the women, men and children standing by the pickup trucks. They did not try to flee. The women held their children close. Some of the men put their hands up in fear of being shot, and surrendered helplessly.

"Nobody move!" the voice from the loudspeaker yelled at them. "Hands up! Everybody hands up! Women, too! Everybody, hands up, dammit! Let's go! Everybody hands up! Women, too!"

Lights as bright as day flooded the area. Now I could clearly see it was not Theresa who stood in the door of the camper holding her baby. It was another girl, hardly older than Theresa. The boy, who had helped her up earlier, stood at the back of the pickup truck with his hands raised. At his feet lay a bag made of blanket material. He was young, as young as I was. Not yet fifteen.

The patrol car I had seen first drove onto the open area. Behind it, there appeared three more vehicles. Six or seven officers from the Immigration Department approached the people at each pickup truck. Some had their pistols out. One held a submachine gun in firing position.

The voice from the loudspeaker shouted that everyone had to step out of both pickup trucks.

"Everybody out! Everybody out of the camper! The girl with the baby first! Get out!"

The people did not risk going against orders. The girl jumped from the bumper, and one of the agents grabbed her by the arm and pulled her with him, away from the others and the boy.

The girl's face was no longer the face of a girl; instead, it had become the face of a despairing mother.

Sirens sounded somewhere in the city. They quickly became louder. I abandoned my hiding place, slipped along the wall and got to the ditch on the other side of the bridge. In the shadow of a tin shed, I crept into the ditch and out of the spotlights. I ran in an easterly direction not knowing where else to run.

*

The boy was watching me from a distance of maybe twenty meters. He sat on a doorless refrigerator. Behind him, dawn was breaking over a mountain of junk. The boy leaned on top of the fridge and smoked a cigarette. He blew out through his nose, and he looked at me through the smoke. I was freezing. It had turned cold while I slept and wind was blowing, causing a loose piece of metal on the shed to squeak. I stood up and tried to shake the cold out of my bones. It didn't work. I couldn't stop shivering.

"You want a cigarette?" the boy asked.

I looked at him.

"Where can you get something to eat around here?"

"To eat?"

"Yes, beans and rice or something. Tortillas."

"On the other side." The boy tilted his head south. Mexico was there. The wall of steel plates was there, which I could not see from here. "On this side, you get breakfast at McDonald's. But only if you have dollars."

"I don't have any."

He grinned. "Maybe you have a revolver."

I reached for the gun, but it was no longer in my pants.

"I had a revolver," I said and went over to a gutted-out car that was lying upside down on its roof. With my back to the boy, I undid my pants and peed against the dented metal fender. I heard him jump down from the refrigerator. When I was finished and turned back to him, he was standing where

I had been sleeping. He reached under his shirt and brought my revolver to light.

"You slept deeply," he said. "Here. I'm giving you back your piece."

He offered the revolver to me. I took it from his hand. "Thanks," I said and put it out of sight under my shirt.

"Someone else would not have only stolen the revolver. Someone else would have put you away for good." He depicted a gun barrel with his finger. "You're lucky I'm someone who has not killed anybody yet. You're lucky nobody from the Barrio Libre Sur, from Flaco's gang, found you here."

"Flaco? You know him?"

"Everybody knows him."

"I don't know him."

"Who do you know?"

"A girl with a cat."

"A girl with a cat?" He looked at me in amazement.

"Do you know a girl with a cat?" I asked him.

He shook his head.

"Too bad," I said. "We were traveling together. Three or four nights ago, we had to separate. Since then, I haven't seen her."

The sun came up, shining on the mountain of junk below. Some of the metal pieces gleamed as if they were gold. I sensed the warmth of the sun on my arms and my face. Then I noticed the boy's peculiar green eyes. In the light, they were as bright as the stones in a necklace my mother used to wear. Polished opals.

"What's your name?" I asked him.

"Alex," he said. "And yours?"

"Santiago."

"And your girl?"

"She's not my girl."

He smiled. "What is the name of the girl with the cat?"

"Lucia."

"Lucia? My friends and I, we will keep a lookout for her."

"Are you a bajador?" I asked. "One of the kids in the tunnels?"

He laughed and shook his head. "My father is a border official. One of the Migra."

I stared at him in disbelief.

"Then you are a gringo."

"My father and my mother came from Mexico. They came to America illegally when they were children. With their parents."

"And now they're Americans?"

"Yes. My father is with the Immigration Service here in the Nogales Sector. My mother is a teacher. She doesn't think the tunnel kids are despicable rats, but instead children who've never experienced love and care. My father has some difficulties with it. He, too, has sympathy for these kids, but that doesn't go well with his job and his sense of duty."

"And you? What do you think?"

"Me?"

"Yes. What do you think of the bajadores?"

He shrugged his narrow shoulders. "That they are a rather lost bunch. No way out."

"Can you take me to Flaco?"

"What do you want from Flaco?"

"Someone gave me his name and thought I should talk with him."

"Who?"

"A woman."

"A woman from the other side?"

"Yes."

"I can imagine who."

"They call her Sarita."

"Just who I thought."

"Will you take me to Flaco?"

He nodded. "Come on. I'll show you where to find him."

I followed him through the junk and into a drainage ditch with tall grass growing on both sides that almost looked like reeds. We went along a narrow footpath on the bottom of the ditch. We scared up a young coyote that seemed to have discovered something on the embankment. He ran away as we appeared. As soon as he noticed we weren't a threat, he stopped to take a better look at us. Alex picked up a stone to throw at the coyote. The young coyote knew what Alex had in mind and ran away on the path. Alex laughed and threw the rock in the direction the coyote had disappeared.

When we got to the place where the coyote had been digging, Alex stopped and looked for something in the thick grass. A trace led from the path up onto the embankment. Many of the shoulder-high blades of grass were bent; some even lay flat on the ground.

"You smell something?" Alex asked.

I nodded. Weakly, I perceived an odor I had last smelled in Chiapas—the smell of a decaying cadaver.

Alex followed the trace and stopped after a few paces.

"Here we are," I heard him say.

"What is it?"

"Come here."

I went after him, and when I got to where he was standing, I saw the man lying in the grass. He was wearing only trousers and an armless undershirt. No shoes. No shirt. He lay on his stomach, his head in our direction and his arms stretched up over his head. Whoever dragged him to this place, left him lying here, with his head crushed to a bloody clump, and his shirt and pants defiled with dried blood. Flies swarmed all around him, and the disgusting stench forced us to put our hands over our noses and mouths.

"A chicken," Alex said in English.

"Un pollo?" I asked.

"Looks that way. That's why he got killed. A chicken getting plucked by a pollero. Coyotes bring people to the border and no further. Polleros slip the people through the tunnels and the holes in the fence. Sometimes the pollos are fleeced by the polleros for money. That' s the way it works around here."

We turned our backs on the corpse and went back to the path.

"We call illegal immigrants chickens or hens. Some of them do not have anything. No money, no valuables. Not even a cheap watch. They're the ones who have to give the coyotes who guide them everything else they have to get securely across the border."

"If they have nothing, they can't give the coyotes anything," I responded.

"At least they still have their dignity. Women and girls are getting raped in the tunnels. For them it is a high price to pay to be free. But there are always some illegals who try to get in on their own because they want to keep their valuables and their money for themselves. They think they would be lucky enough to get through. When they realize that this is not a lottery game they can win, they suck up to the children who live in the tunnels. Children belonging to Flaco's gang, or to another. These people never have a chance, because the children are not children."

"The children are not children?"

"No. The children are like you."

"And how am I?"

"Dangerous," he said and smiled.

"Unpredictable."

"That's all right," I conceded. It made me proud a guy like him considered me dangerous.

Alex laughed as if he had guessed my thoughts.

"You are not alone, Santiago," he said. "You are just one of many. You will fit in well around here."

"And you?"

"Me? I am at home here, now that I am in their world." He turned his back to me and pushed on.

We reached a tunnel. Someone had torn an iron grating from its casement, and the entrance to the tunnel was open. Alex stopped about twenty paces from the tunnel.

"What's this?" I asked him.

"From here on, you go alone," he said.

"Are you afraid of Flaco?"

To my surprise, he nodded. "Yes. I don't want to cross paths with him."

"Why not? What's he done to you?"

"Nothing. But I know what Flaco's done to other people."

"What other people?"

"Ask him. He'll maybe tell you."

"If you come with me, I'll make sure nothing happens to you," I said. "That, I promise you. You know I have this gun. And it's loaded."

He grinned at me. "If you should need me, ask the children. But do not ask for Alex. When you ask for me, you have to ask for Sombra."

Was that his nickname? I studied him carefully. He was a delicate boy, almost as delicate as a girl.

"Sombra?" I said. "Like a shadow?"

"I am that," he said, laughing. "My name is Alex, but when you see me, you see only a shadow. My father's name is Alex, and he wanted a son."

105

I had no idea what he meant. Maybe something wasn't quite right in his head.

Then he raised his T-shirt, and my knees went weak when I saw his breasts.

"You… you are…"

He laughed, turned around and gracefully ran away.

For a long moment, I stood on the path, incapable of forming a clear thought. Alex was not a boy. Not with those breasts. I wanted to call him back, but he had already disappeared somewhere in the ditches. I had never before met a boy who was not a boy. At home, I had heard of a girl who was not a girl. Some people sometimes made fun of it. Made nasty jokes. I never saw this girl because she lived in a different village and didn't often let herself be seen.

"Hey."

The shout tore me out of my thoughts. I turned around and was standing opposite a boy and a girl who had come out of the tunnel. The girl was clutching a pistol, pointing it at me.

"I want to see Flaco," I said.

"Who wants to see Flaco?" the girl asked.

"Me."

"Who are you?"

"My name is Santiago."

They looked at me.

"Who brought you here?" asked the boy.

"Sombra," I said.

The girl laughed disdainfully. "What do you want from Flaco?"

"That is something I will tell him, not you."

They exchanged a quick glance.

"Also, not far from here, there's a dead chicken. Any time now, someone will discover it."

"Where's the dead chicken?"

"About five hundred paces from here, lying in the grass."

"We'll take it away tonight," said the girl. "Come on."

The boy asked me once again where the corpse lay. Without concerning himself further with the girl or me, he went down the path in the direction I'd indicated. The girl motioned to me with a hand to follow her. She disappeared into the tunnel, and I climbed over a few bent and rusty iron rods along the way and followed her. She lit the way into the tunnel with a flashlight.

*

The tunnel ran slightly uphill from Nogales, Arizona, beneath the border, and all the way to Nogales, Sonora. It wasn't the same tunnel I'd gone through to get to America the night before. When going back, this tunnel ended in a concrete canal leading through the middle of the city on the Mexican side.

The girl, who hadn't wanted to tell me her name, led me through a part of the city where there were all sorts of small street shops. The stores offered lots of souvenirs and other plunder to the tourists who came across the border by the hundreds every day and bought colorful tablecloths and leather bags and Aztec gods made of plaster. It was early in the morning, and most of these little shops were still closed. Nonetheless, there were already a few ragged women squatting on the edges of the street with their ragged little children. Indian women, from villages in the mountains, who had been sent to the border by their men to sell trinkets, or to just beg for money.

At a crossing, a man was setting up his donkey and cart. Later, for a few pesos, he would use a Polaroid camera to photograph gringos sitting in the donkey cart. The donkey wore a hat with two holes his long ears poked through.

I stopped at a newsstand and bought myself a newspaper. The girl watched me suspiciously.

"What do you want with a newspaper?" she asked.

"I am going to read it," I said.

The girl closed her eyes tightly. "You can read?" The same question Don Fernando had asked me.

"Yes."

We went on. I held the paper rolled up in my hand. A patrol car drove near us on the street. Very slowly. The two police officers looked at us. At the next crossing, the patrol car stopped. One of the officers climbed out and placed himself in our path.

"Where did you get that newspaper from?" he asked.

"He bought it," said the girl.

"I don't believe you," said the police officer and stretched out his hand. "Give me that paper, boy. "

I handed the newspaper to him. He thanked me, climbed into the patrol car and they drove away.

"Why did you give him the paper?" the girl asked.

"What else could I do?" I said. "Should I have killed him?"

"There certainly wouldn't be any mourning for that dirtbag."

"You know him, then?"

"I know them all, the filthy pigs," said the girl. "I've slept with some of them. They'll leave us alone." We went up the street, which now climbed steeply, broken asphalt full of cracks and potholes. The buildings stood crookedly against one another on both sides of the street. Colorfully painted houses, blue and turquoise and pink. Dogs wandered around. Children and elderly people watched us.

"Now you have no newspaper to read," said the girl.

It sounded as if she was sorry I had let the officer take the newspaper away from us.

"I will buy another one. Maybe tomorrow."

"Tomorrow? Won't there be something new of importance in it, different than today?"

"Yes."

"Then maybe you should buy today's newspaper again."

"Yes, we'll see."

"I've never read a newspaper."

"Have you ever read a book?"

"No." The girl looked at me. "You?"

I nodded. "The Adventures of Tom Sawyer."

"Who's that?"

"A boy in America. He lived over a hundred years ago."

"Was he really alive or did he just live in a writer's fantasies?"

"That I don't know. Maybe both. Maybe the writer knew a boy like him and wrote a story about him."

The girl led me through a narrow alley between houses and then through a side door into a room painted blue and white. The door stood open. From the door frame hung a curtain made of string. The room was small and dark. An old woman sat at a table checking out beans in a flat basket. She sorted out a few bad ones and laid them on the table.

"Is Flaco here, Señora?" asked the girl.

The old woman raised her head. Her wrinkled face was almost black. She wore eyeglasses that had only one lens. She had a cloth wrapped around her head.

"Who are you bringing there?" she asked in a croaking voice. "You're not to bring anyone here; this is my home."

"Lovely home," said the girl. "This here, this is Santiago. He's from Chiapas, and he can read."

The old woman looked at me with one eye, studying me through the frame with no lens. She wheezed deeply through her nose, then she pointed to a door with a crooked index finger. The girl knocked.

"Flaco. It's me, Nila."

I heard a few strange sounds behind the door. Nila opened the door and motioned me to follow her. The room behind the door was smaller still. Some human bodies lay on the floor, tangled up in one another. It smelled of feces and vomit. A torn cloth hung over the window. Nila went in, took the rag down and opened the window.

"God, it's a miracle you haven't suffocated in here," she said.

A boy about my age or a little older heaved himself up and looked at me. He was skin and bones, a skeleton, his face wilted.

"This is Flaco," said Nila. Flaco wanted to say something, but he doubled over cramping, and he vomited. Afterward, he sat bent over between the other kids for a while, with his head hanging. He didn't move anymore.

Nila looked at me and nodded toward some spray paint cans and plastic bags lying on the floor.

"Inhaled too much of this shit," she said. "It'll take a few minutes until it's all been puked up."

Flaco raised his head. "Don't give me that shit, bitch," he said. Out of teary eyes he stared at me and wiped the vomit from his mouth and chin with the back of his hand. "Who are you?" he asked me.

"My name is Santiago," I said.

"Where are you from?"

"Chiapas."

"Chiapas? Did you fight there?"

"My father did. He was a Zapatista."

"And?"

"They killed him."

"And you?"

"What about me?"

"What do you want here? You are one of the Indians down there. They do not just go away."

"I am a Tzotzil."

"A Tzotzil?" He laughed. "You look like a damned Indian to me."

I said nothing.

"What do you want here?" he asked again.

"They told me there is money to be made here."

"Here?" He scratched the back of his head. "Who told you that?"

"I heard it often while traveling. Lots of talk about it. About the tunnels."

"Have you told him this shit, Nila?"

"Yeah, you think I'm an idiot, dammit. The only thing I want is to get out of here, go to California. But before I go, I'll pull the wool over your gummy eyes, Flaco."

He bared his yellow teeth in a grin. "She has no respect," he said. "Not for anybody. Not even me. Someone should wring her neck."

"Just try it," Nila snapped. "You wouldn't be the first one I wasted, you prick."

"She has friends among the cops," Flaco explained to me.

"Without my friends, you would've been done in long ago."

"That's true." Flaco got up and kicked a boy lying near him in the ribs. "They can't take anything, these jerks," he said. "And they don't have any self-esteem left in them, living like pigs. Let's go outside for some fresh air. I'm sick of the stink in here."

We went out between the houses back to the street.

"Where are we going?" I asked.

"Down there," he said. "Into the city."

We went as a trio back down the steep street Nila and I had climbed up.

"The last thing anyone who's made it this far wants to do is stay here," Flaco said without looking at me. "They all want to go to Hollywood and fuck Marilyn Monroe. But she's been dead for decades, Jesus Christ."

"I've never thought about fucking Marilyn Monroe," I said.

Nila laughed. "And me?"

"Not you either."

Flaco laughed. "I like you, man. Don't let yourself like anything about her."

We all three laughed. Then we sat on a bench in a small park not far from where Tomo had been killed. And we watched the people. The park was full of trash. A statue stood in its center. Behind the park, the canal ran by.

"The cops took a newspaper away from Santiago that he had bought," said Nila.

"What you want with a dumbass newspaper?" asked Flaco. "You know what newspapers are good for? To wipe your ass with, that's what. Or to wrap a stinking fish you'll eat later."

"He reads the newspaper, Flaco," Nila said, and it sounded almost as if she was admiring me.

"What about your ass? Don't you wipe it?"

"How can someone earn money here?" I asked him.

"You can wait until you run into a chicken with money. Then you knock him in the head with a lead pipe and take his money."

"And how else? Killing chicken is not a passion of mine."

"There's one lying very close to our tunnel," said Nila.

"What are you talking about?" Flaco asked.

"A dead guy with his head beaten in is lying there. Santiago found him. I sent Diego to have a look. It would be better if we put the chicken somewhere else."

"Who did him in?"

"No idea. None of us, apparently."

"Maybe the cops. Then they put his body near our tunnel, so it looks like we killed him."

The patrol car drove by, the two cops and my newspaper. They looked at us and grinned.

"Fuckass pigs," Flaco said between clenched teeth. "Say, do you have any coin?"

"Not many."

"Give Nila some. She can buy us a Coke."

"Buy your own Coke, dammit," Nila snarled.

"Give her some change, my friend."

I gave Nila a little of my money, and she left the park. I thought she would never come back again. But, after ten minutes, she was back with two bottles.

"Here," she said and gave me back a few coins. I put them in my pocket. Flaco and I drank our ice-cold Cokes.

"If you want to stay here, I'll make you my adjutant," Flaco said suddenly.

Nila raised her head.

I looked over at the main street where the people were streaming by, many of them tourists. They all seemed to be going somewhere, in one direction or another. I had heard what Flaco said, but my thoughts were with Lucia.

I thought I could magically bring her here, if I could only think of her strongly enough or wished for her hard enough. That's why I stared at the people. Sometimes I was sure I saw her, but whenever I was about to jump up, I would see that it wasn't her.

"Did you hear what he said, Santiago?" asked Nila.

"Yes."

"And?"

"I ask myself why I should be his adjutant."

"Because he's the king," said Nila.

"The king of what?"

"The king of the empire," she said mockingly. "Feared and respected at the same time." She laughed. "Without him, nothing happens here. Right, Flaco?"

"What?"

"Nothing happens here without your consent."

"Consent?" Flaco asked. "What the hell is that?"

"It means you decide if something happens or not," Nila explained.

"Not much," Flaco admitted modestly. "Still, I didn't know about a death chicken lying near my tunnel."

"You're still the king, Flaco."

"I am the king, dammit." Flaco threw his empty bottle at the memorial pedestal of a statue. The bottle exploded and covered the ground with shards of glass.

"And why should you trust me?" I asked him. "You don't know me."

"I'm a student of people," he said, and he stood up. "Right, Nila?"

"Oh, yes, he is a student of people," she affirmed sarcastically.

"Nila is the only one I can't figure out," he said. "She is a deceiving bitch."

Nila kicked at him, but he expertly evaded her foot.

"I need a gun," he continued. "A pistol. Nothing special. Just a cheap gun for someone who wants to do away with his old lady."

"Give him yours," said Nila.

"Mine? You're crazy. I cherish my gun."

"Then get one from T.T.," Nila suggested. "For sure, he has one he would sell to you."

"And the money?" Flaco asked. "Do you have the money, bitch?"

"Don't talk to me like that. It's not proper for a king to talk like that."

"Well, do you have the money to buy a gun, my dear?"

"Not me," she smiled. "But Santiago has the money. Right, Santiago?"

I looked at her darkly. "My money is my money," I said.

Flaco laughed aloud. "I like you, man. You do not take any shit from her. That is why she wants to have sex with you. To make you her dog."

"Better I lay with him than with you, Flaco," Nila answered coldly. "He's not infested with lice."

Flaco sat next to me and placed his arm on my shoulders.

"If you want to make money, this is your first opportunity. I'll tell you where you can easily get a gun you can resell to my customer. No middle man. You do it alone. I want none of the money, understand?"

"Why are you doing this?"

"It is, so to speak, my welcome into my empire, a present for you. So you know you can trust me. I will trust you, my friend. Together, we are a strong team. Together, we are undefeatable."

"He said the same thing to Tomo," said Nila. "I was there when he said it. But Tomo's been murdered and now he's afraid they'll get him, too."

"Who's Tomo?" I asked, though I well knew who Tomo had been.

"Tomo was his adjutant. Yesterday, he was stabbed and shot. Nobody knows who did it. He was so full of cuts and holes there had to be more than one of them. And now the king is afraid he's next in line. Right, Flaco?"

"Don't talk crap, Nila."

"I'm not talking crap, and you know it," Nila sneered. "He's afraid because he doesn't know who killed Tomo. Maybe it was the cops. Perhaps it was one of Bernardo's people. Maybe it was a tramp or someone who had an old score to settle. You are losing your grip on your empire, Flaco."

"Don't talk crap, Nila, " Flaco snapped again. "I have no more credit with T.T. If Santiago goes to him, he'll get a gun, and he'll make at least fifty bucks for profit. Fifty bucks, clear. That's no peanuts, man. That's genuine fuckin' U.S. dollars, you understand. I insist guns be paid in U.S. dollars. That's my rule."

"And where do I find this T.T.?"

"On the other side. Nila can bring you there."

"I am not going there. Not now, not after what happened to Tomo."

"Look who's full of shit," Flaco said and laughed. He pulled Nila close and slapped her on the butt. "I also don't have lice, darling. Never had any. Come on, let's go to the tunnel and see what's going on."

We left the park. On the way, Flaco bought me a newspaper.

"So you can wipe your ass," he said, laughing.

*

Diego was waiting for us at the entrance of the tunnel. His head was shaved clean, his teeth were a mess and his arms were covered with tattoos. He sat in the tunnel with a Walkman in his lap and headphones on. As we approached, he took off the headphones and turned off the Walkman. Out of respect for Flaco.

"Hey, Flaco," he said as the Walkman disappeared under his shirt.

"Hey," Flaco said. "What about the dead chicken?"

"Plucked clean," said Diego. "I carried him to the bridge and laid him in the shadows there. Either the cops or the coyotes will find him first." Flaco pointed at me with his thumb. "This is the new guy," he said. "For Tomo."

Diego looked at me silently with respect. I sensed it. This kid was a bastard through and through, but he paid attention to me.

"I think Tomo was okay," he said.

"Tomo was okay," said Nila.

"Sure he was okay," said Flaco. It sounded like the beginning of a funeral sermon nobody wanted to end. They all thought about Tomo. I thought about Lucia, amazed at myself because I thought of her almost every moment. Such a thing had never happened to me before, and it somehow made me nervous.

"What are you thinking of?" Nila asked me.

"Nothing," I said.

"Not so," she said with a smile. "I bet you're thinking about a girl."

I laughed aloud and at the same time, I was amazed I was denying it.

"What's her name?" Nila asked me.

"Leave it alone, dammit. He doesn't want to screw you, okay? And you have nothing to say about it. You don't have the least thing to say about..."

"And you'd be better off keeping your mouth shut, Flaco," she interrupted. "You'd be better off thinking about what it means that Tomo got killed. Maybe you're in someone's way. Or maybe Tomo ran his own game behind your back. It could also be the cops want to clean out the tunnels again and drive away all the rats."

Flaco's dark eyes were shining. "They've threatened it often enough, especially the gringo cops." He turned to me and said: "Once, they barred both tunnels with these iron gratings. We tore them all out."

"Lately, too many chickens got killed," explained Nila.

"Every other day somebody finds one. We all know it can't go on much longer."

"There aren't enough cops to drive us out," Flaco said. "More cops, that costs a lot of money. The good citizens' tax money, that is. So the politicians would rather wait and pray that we all kill each other off, and the problem will solve itself."

"All the same," said Nila. "They won't just passively watch, for better or worse."

"We haven't killed a chicken in a long time," said Diego. "The last one Tomo killed more than a month ago. But Tomo and I buried him there on the other side. Nobody found him."

"Who sent you here?" Flaco suddenly asked me, mistrust in his eyes.

"Sarita," I said.

"The old lady at the Hotel Camino Real?"

"Yes."

Flaco looked at Nila and Nila looked at me.

"She pays us for the people she sends through our tunnel," she said. "Lots of polleros work for her. Tomo once was one of Sarita's polleros."

"Maybe she doesn't want to pay any more?" I said.

"I don't believe that," said Nila.

"I don't trust anyone anymore," said Flaco.

"History tells us this usually is the beginning of the end of all empires, Flaco," Nila told him.

"Keep your mouth shut, Nila!" he yelled.

"You trust him," said Diego, pointing to me.

"The new guy's okay," said Flaco. "You better be sure about it, Diego." He looked at Nila and pointed at her. "As for you, you can't be sure of anything, Nila. Maybe you're on Bernardo's list—maybe you're on mine."

"Don't forget the cops, Flaco. If something happens to me, they'll get Bernardo or you. Or both of you."

We followed the path along a ravine and climbed through a hole in the border fence to the other side where the dead chicken had been. The high grass was trampled down. Although the corpse was no longer there, I saw it, and I could still smell it.

*

"Grand Avenue," said Flaco, as if the concrete canal were a road paved with gold leading us directly to Hollywood. He pointed to a tunnel opening at least twenty steps wide and three or four meters high. The concrete walls covered with graffiti and a thin trickle ran between clumps of garbage. A girl cowered there next to a tire, washing a T-shirt in a red plastic bucket.

We looked out for patrol cars, but there were none to be seen. We weren't able to detect anything suspicious or dangerous. So we climbed down into the canal.

"The kids come here from everywhere," said Flaco. "Like you, most of them are from the south, some from Guatemala or from even farther south, from Bolivia. Most of them are just drifters with nothing to lose. No fear of anything, not even dying, my friend."

We approached the tunnel entrance. The girl looked up from her work. She was young, maybe twelve or thirteen and her upper lip was swollen and crusted with blood.

"Who was it, Angela?" Nila asked the girl.

"Jorge and Felix. They were fighting over me, and when I wanted to separate them, Jorge hit me with his fist."

"You should go away from here, Angela," Nila suggested.

The girl shook her head. "It's okay," she said.

Flaco and I went on. When we reached the entrance, he looked around for Nila who was crouching by a girl who rested her head on Nila's shoulder.

"She has a good heart," said Flaco. "One day she'll pay for it."

The bajadores lived in the tunnel in the midst of the junk they brought in. They stared at us out of their dark, glittering eyes. It was as if they were waiting for a command. Some stood leaning against the walls. Others lay on old mattresses and under dirty blankets. Spray cans and small plastic sacks lay everywhere. A boy sitting on a split automobile seat sprayed fumes from a spray can into a see-through plastic sack, and put it quickly to his mouth to suck the chemicals deep into his lungs. He inhaled again and again until the plastic sack hung from his hands.

And Flaco, he was the king. He went around with his chest puffed out, his head high and he looked everyone in the eyes. Directly in the eyes. And they would have fallen to their knees had he demanded it of them.

I was proud to be at his side. The king and his adjutant.

"This is Santiago," he said to a boy who lay with a girl on a mattress. I had never seen a girl's face more made up than hers and her hair styled to a wild mane. She looked at me and smiled. The boy looked right through me.

"This is Santiago," said Flaco a few more times to those who were standing and lying around. Sometimes he would stop and call a boy to him and ask how business was going. And he would say things like: "Do something for me, man, and I'll make sure things go well for you."

They believed him. They believed in his power, and they believed he was there for them. The only person in the world who was there for them.

"If you want to fuck a girl, then tell me," he said as we went deeper into the tunnel. "Most of the ones here are sick. Some have HIV. Most of them have the clap. If you want a girl, then we'll go somewhere else, my friend."

I didn't want a girl. Not now and not later. I wanted to see Lucia again. Nothing else.

Suddenly, he stopped because seven or eight boys and a girl stepped out of the tunnel and came toward us, putting themselves in our path. The girl was about fourteen or fifteen years old. One of the boys seemed to be about ten, and the others were not much older.

"This is Santiago," Flaco said to them. "Where are you going?"

"Somebody wasted Tomo," said one of them, wearing a black bandana around his head and a T-shirt with the sleeves torn off. "We want to find out who it was."

"Then tell me who it was," answered Flaco. "If I know who's responsible, I'll take decisive measures."

The way he spoke was also what made him king.

"At this point, all we know is that it was not Bernardo's people," said a boy.

Flaco laid a hand on his shoulder and said: "You should not trust anyone, Benito. Not even your brother." Then he pointed to me. "This here, this is our new adjutant. His name is Santiago. You can trust him because he is my right hand."

They looked at me.

"Why him?" one of them asked. "Why not Diego?"

"I made my decision," said Flaco. "Any objections, Ponciano?"

Nobody objected. They let us pass, and we went deeper into the tunnel, where it got dark. At one spot, marked on the wall with a white line and a brass measurement placket, Flaco said here, directly above us, was the border. "Earlier, everybody crossed the border above and through the fence. Then the gringos started putting up this wall made of steel, and there are only few places left where there's a fence. Since then, more and more try to get through the tunnels. Illegals,

121

smugglers, everybody who wants to cross the border."

Flaco flashed his light over somebody lying crumpled up on the floor next to a grocery cart, half covered by a torn blanket.

"That is Nando," said Flaco. "He is sick."

"From sniffing the paint?" I asked.

Flaco went over to the boy and illuminated his face. Nando was emaciated, and his eyes lay sunken in dark holes.

"Nando," said Flaco and pushed the boy with his foot. The boy didn't move. As we went on, Flaco told me the boy's story and why he'd been sick for several weeks.

"The cops did him in. He raped a girl in one of the tunnels. The girl defended herself. Nando beat her for it, using a piece of roofing tile. Later, the girl crawled out of the tunnel, and the cops from Grupo Beta picked her up. Nando knew nothing. He inhaled enough fumes from spray paint cans he believed he was sitting on the moon looking down on the world. The cops waited outside for him. For two or three days. When he came out, they snapped him up and took him to headquarters. And there, they worked him over like they'd never done anyone before."

"What did they do to him? "

"I don't know whether you want to hear this, man. It's an awful story."

"Tell me."

"In the prison cell, they ordered him to dance with another guy and to kiss him. Then they forced the older guy to rape Nando."

As we walked on I kept quiet. I sensed the rage and the hate swell up in me, and I thought about the captain I'd shot, and I felt no regret. Then I thought of Lucia and her torn dress. I wished I could have protected her when she had to flee from the men. I wished I'd been there and had killed both of them with my revolver.

"It makes me want to vomit," said Flaco. "Instead of helping Nando, they made everything much worse. Instead of helping him, they've wrecked him."

"How could they have helped him?" I asked.

He didn't answer.

"We can't expect anyone to help any of us," I said. "Because we are what we are, we have to help ourselves."

"The world makes us into what we are."

"The world?"

"Those who give the orders in this world. Those who have all the money and all the land and all the power. There is nothing left over for us except some pocket money we can steal from other poor suckers. And sometimes, we kill one of them rich people, and they call it murder, but, for us, it's pretty near justice."

"There is no justice."

"But things are not going so badly for us, my friend. We're alive. That kid there, he's dying a horrible death, man."

Flaco pulled out a pack of cigarettes and lit one up.

"I still believe that there's no justice," I said. "Not here and not in another world."

"There is no other."

"I mean after death."

"After death, there is nothing."

"How do you know?"

"Nobody knows that. But I don't believe there is anything after death. There was nothing before I was born. And there will be nothing after I die."

"You don't know that."

"No."

We were quiet.

"But what you say does make sense," I said after a while. "All who are responsible for what happens in this world are also responsible for Nando, who once was just a child, one who gradually turned into what he'll be when he dies."

Flaco stopped midstride.

"We're talking a pile of shit," he said. "I don't think of these things often. My understanding doesn't function very well anymore. It's from the spray paint. Sometimes I wonder if I should just shoot a bullet into my head. But then I think again; life's not that bad. Not as damned bad as Nando's life, anyway. He's nearly done with his, hanging onto a thread. Ever since he came back, he just lies there. I think he'll be dead in a few days, from hunger and thirst."

"Someone should tell him to get a grip on his life."

"Who should tell him?"

"I don't know. Somebody."

"Who?"

"No idea." The boy who was a girl occurred to me. "Maybe Sombra," I said.

He moved his head around. "Sombra?"

"Yes, he led me to your tunnel."

"He is not a he, man," Flaco laughed.

"I know that."

"Where did you notice?"

"I just know it."

We walked on.

"We're talking a pile of shit," he said again. "I thought you were rough and cold as a dog's nose. But I believe I've made a mistake with you."

"No, you haven't."

He laughed aloud. "And how so?"

"I've shot a cop," I said.

"Don't talk shit, man."

It got brighter up ahead. We were approaching the end of the tunnel. Also, here in the half shadows, kids had nested.

They stared at us as we approached.

"Hey," Flaco shouted at them. "This here is Santiago. He comes from Chiapas and the soldiers killed his father. I've made him my adjutant to replace Tomo."

"Somebody knows who killed Tomo?" asked a girl who sat between two other girls and had a baby in her arms.

"The cops," said a boy nearby, his upper arm tattooed up to over his shoulder with the words Barrio Libre Sur. Below it was a cross and a bleeding heart. An older kid with needles in his hand was there to tattoo a crown of thorns onto the boy's brown skin.

"That's José, our artist," Flaco said. "Most of the better graffiti in the canals and the tunnels are his. But he has also made a real picture, a mural on the wall of a church. They showed it even in the newspaper."

"If you want to look at it, you'll have to go to the Church of San Miguel," said José as he inspected the points of the two needles he had dipped in a small container of black India ink.

"Want to have a tattoo, man?" he asked me. "'Viva Zapata' and a bullet for your father?"

"Perhaps another time," I answered, wondering how he knew the fate of my father. I figured there must be talk about me in the streets and the tunnels.

Another boy gestured Flaco to come to him. The two of them put their heads together and talked with each other. I sat down in the canal in the sun and read my newspaper. The kids watched me. Some had plastic bags in their fists and snorted spray paint. One of them came over.

"What's in it?" he asked, pointing at the newspaper.

"A professor says we humans are destroying the world."

He laughed. His voice sounded scratchy from the spray paint propellant he'd inhaled, wrecking his vocal cords. He offered me his plastic bag.

I shook my head.

"Try it," he urged me. "It's not going to kill you, just a little bit of lacquer in it."

I took the plastic bag from his hands and held it so the vapor couldn't escape.

"Try it," he said again.

I put the plastic bag to my mouth and relaxed my grip a bit. A repulsive, corrosive smell went from my mouth to my nose. I tried to inhale the vapor from the bag, but before I could take a real pull from it, a coughing fit overcame me. I couldn't get any more air. I opened my mouth wide and jumped to my feet. The plastic bag fell out of my hand and, still struggling for breath, I staggered around as if I were drunk. I heard the kids laughing, and someone held me quick by the arm. I tore myself loose and fell to my knees. My burning eyes began to tear, and I thought I was going to smother. Then I heard Flaco's voice drowning everything out.

"You damned bastard," he roared. I turned my head and saw through a veil of tears how he grabbed a baseball bat and went after the kid who'd given me the bag. The kid raised both arms to defend himself, but the baseball bat hit him from the side, and he tumbled down the canal. Flaco followed him, yelling at him and beat him down. And when the kid lay on the ground, Flaco stood over him and raised the baseball bat for a last blow.

"Stop, Flaco," I coughed and, although I scarcely had a voice, he heard it. He turned his head and stared at me with wild eyes. I was kneeling in a mud puddle a few steps away from him, and I raised a hand. I had to support myself with the other one; otherwise, I would have fallen on my face.

"I'm okay," I said. "Leave him alone.

He couldn't understand; he couldn't understand I wanted to stop him from bashing in the kid's head. He slowly let the baseball bat sink and took a step away. I raised myself up and came to my feet. The kid still lay on the dirty cement. His nose was bleeding.

Flaco shook the baseball bat at him, but he didn't hit him.

"Come on," he shouted at me, and he went away down the canal. After he'd calmed down, I asked him why he'd lost control of himself.

"I don't want you to go to waste too, dammit," he said. "Right now, I can't put up with this shit. At least one of us has to have a clear head, do you understand?"

I didn't know what he meant, but I didn't ask him any more questions.

*

I met with the man at night. That was how Flaco arranged it. There were no streetlights at our meeting place and because there was no moon, the only light came from the stars.

He stood in the shadow of the San Miguel Church in front of the mural José had painted.

I had no idea who the man was. To me, he was someone wanting to buy a gun and having the money to do so. One hundred dollars. That was the price for a gun, no matter what brand or caliber. "Don't get involved," Flaco warned me. "The man wants a revolver. No questions asked. No complications. A hundred dollars. Gringo money. No pesos. A Smith & Wesson costs the same as a Colt 45 or a .38 caliber Saturday night special. Only small caliber guns are a little cheaper, but nobody wants any of those, except for .22 automatics, but they're not so easy to come by."

The man knew nothing about handguns. "Do you have the revolver?" he asked without showing me his face.

"No. In the first place, I don't walk around carrying a gun, and secondly, I need a down payment first."

The man was uncertain. I sensed it clearly. No, I smelled it. He stank like a dog. I knew this smell. Sweat. People who are afraid smell this way, as if they're sweating piss through their pores. He was a decent man who had some account to settle, and to do what he wanted to do, just this, smooth and easy, he needed a gun that came from the other side. And that later, in case it was found, could not be traced back to the owner.

"I can't wait much longer," the man said nervously. "It has to be done quick."

"When I have the down payment, it will go quickly."

"When?"

"Tomorrow night. Same time as now. At the same place."

"How much?"

"A hundred dollars. In American dollars. I don't take pesos."

"And the down payment?"

"Half of that."

The man rummaged around in his pockets, brought out a wallet and took out a few bills.

"Here," said the man. "Two twenties and a ten."

"Good." I stuck the money in the pocket of my jeans.

"Then… then I'll see you tomorrow."

"Yes."

"And one more thing…"

"What?"

"Not a small caliber one, please."

I left him without a word.

*

There were several possible ways for me to get to the other side. The simplest way was to use one of the two tunnels I already knew. First, I went to the Hotel Camino Real and watched the front entrance for a while.

At least two dozen men came and went. I couldn't be sure whether everyone who went into the hotel also left through the front door. I didn't know who the men were. Perhaps they were coyotes who wanted to buy an illegal passage to American territory for their customers. Or drug smugglers trying to get a load of pot through one of the gaps in the iron wall. A patrol car stopped in front of the hotel. One of the two police officers went inside and came back out a little while later. The patrol car drove off.

Flaco's words so deeply etched into my memory; I would probably never forget them. "You cannot trust anyone. Nobody outside the tunnels and not even the kids in the tunnels." There were corrupt cops and border officials on both sides. And snitches, who informed whoever needed information for a few bucks or for lesser favors. In Gringo-Land, there were but a few, but down in Mexico, almost all government people were corrupt because the whole system there was corrupt.

I watched the patrol car drive away, and I went across the street and behind the hotel. I crouched in the shadow of a half-collapsed wall, and I waited. Nothing happened. Nobody came out. Lights were on in some of the rooms. After midnight, I slipped up to one of the windows, behind which reddish light shimmered. A naked woman lay on the bed, and a man knelt over her. The man had his hairy back turned to me, and I heard him laugh. The woman saw me, but her eyes did not widen even a little. She said nothing to the man, and he let himself down upon her, and she writhed under him as if he were there to strangle her.

I saw the woman's face and eyes in my mind as I went through the night and then through one of the tunnels. I thought of

Lucia and imagined her naked before me; her wonderfully beautiful body and her soft skin I touched with my lips. I quickly put those thoughts through the grinder, because I was sure I would never see her again, much less naked.

Somewhere in the tunnel, someone tried to stop me.

"I am Santiago," I quietly said. "Flaco's adjutant."

I said it to everyone who wanted to stop me, but I was ready, if necessary, to pull out the revolver under my shirt.

A girl followed me.

"Where are you going?" she asked.

I did not answer.

"Can I go with you?"

"No."

The girl stopped. At the end of the tunnel, a small fire burned. Flaco hunkered there on the ground, along with Nila.

He only recognized me when I stood before him and José, the artist, shone a light on my face.

"Do you have the dough for the gun?" Flaco asked me. His eyes were glossed as if he had a fever. He was full of cheap booze and fumes from glue, lacquer, and spray paint. Diego and a couple of others had robbed a small store in Nogales, Arizona, in broad daylight, and they had taken all the spray cans that were there.

Nila got up and took me by the arm.

"I'm going with him," she said.

Flaco laughed and showed her the finger.

"Fuck you, bitch," he said.

We left the tunnel and the canal. Nila held my arm, and we went through the empty streets north of the border. In some of the shops, the display windows were illuminated. Cars drove by and there was no one to be seen anywhere.

"They all disappear at night," Nila explained. "People here are afraid of us."

"Right," I said. "They should fear us."

"One day, they will exterminate us," she said, "like roaches."

We looked at the junk in the show window of a shop. In the midst of the rubbish lay a doll.

"I had one of those once," said Nila. "This one looks almost exactly like mine did."

"Do you want it?"

"Yes, but it has to cost a few dollars."

"I'll buy it for you tomorrow," I said.

She gave me a kiss. I thought of Lucia and as we walked on I wiped off the cheek Nila's lips had touched.

*

Nila led me to a bar that belonged to a gringo named Tom Tucker. He called himself T.T. and his bar was T.T.'s Saloon. "Very original," Nila joked. Supposedly, Tucker had been a cop in Texas. Nobody knew what had happened, but rumor said he killed a black man who resisted arrest. To prevent a scandal, he got fired and moved to Nogales and set up his bar.

We approached the bar from the back.

Nila didn't want to go in. "It's better if he doesn't see me. Tell him Tomo sent you to him."

"Tomo?"

"He got on well with Tomo. For some time Flaco and T.T. have had business difficulties…"

"Flaco owes him money, I bet. And Tomo is dead. What happens if I don't get a gun from him?"

"Show him the money and he'll sell you his soul for it, Santiago."

"His soul for fifty dollars?"

"Or less."

I stood, undecided, in the darkened parking lot and looked

131

at the back entrance, where there was a motorcycle parked next to a garbage.

"What are you waiting for," said Nila. "Knock on the door three times. Didi will let you in."

"Who's Didi?"

"His old lady."

I inhaled the warm night air. It smelled like rain. "Do you smell it too?" I asked Nila.

"What?"

"It smells like rain."

"Maybe the rainy season is beginning." She looked up at the sky. No moon. No clouds. Only an ocean of stars. Like glimmering dust someone had blown into the air.

"I'll wait for you here," she said.

I went to the iron door and knocked. Didi opened it. She was a fat middle-aged woman with huge breasts. She studied me with her little eyes that were almost invisible behind folds of fat.

"Tomo sent me," I said immediately.

"And who the fuck are you?" she asked in English. "A fuckin' Indian?"

"My name is Santiago," I answered in Spanish.

She let me come in and, as the door fell closed behind me, she grabbed my balls as a greeting. A good grip. "Little fella, it won't be long until you're a man," she said in perfect Spanish.

"What then?"

"Then come and see me, kid."

"You belong to T.T.," I said.

"The bar here and all its furnishings belong to T.T. Do I look like an easy chair to you?"

"No."

"Then I don't belong to him."

We went through a narrow hallway past the men's room,

where a guy was leaning against the wall pissing on his cowboy boots and then she had me wait in the kitchen. A gigantic cockroach quickly retreated between the tiles when it saw me. I opened the refrigerator. On a plate inside lay the bloodless head of a pig. T.T. came into the kitchen, and I closed the refrigerator door.

He was a large man with a bull neck and large hands he wiped on an apron as he took my measure.

"Didi says Tomo sent you?" He spoke Spanish, but with a strong American accent, so I had to guess most of what he said.

"That's right," I said.

"Strange part is that Tomo is dead, kid."

"He told me to see you before he got wasted."

He grinned. "You're a smart kid. What's your name?"

"Santiago."

"Where are you from?"

"Chiapas."

"Did you fight there?"

"I didn't."

"Your father?"

"Yes."

"Terrible, the shit happening down there."

I kept silent.

"I don't like any damned Indians, understand? No Sioux and no Apaches and also no damned Navajos. What tribe of prairie niggers do you belong to, kid?"

"I am a Maya."

"A Maya? There haven't been any of those assholes for centuries. They were wiped out by the Spaniards."

"I am a descendant of the Mayas, but people call us Tzotzil."

"Tzotzil? Never heard of them. No clue something like that even existed in our world, kid. Doesn't say much about my education, I guess, but I went to a whole bunch of schools to the bitter end." He laughed. "And what do you want from me, kid?"

"A gun," I said without hesitation.

His glance slid over me. Even though I had stuck my revolver in the back of my waistband, it didn't escape him that I was armed.

"You already have a gun," he said.

"Who says so?"

"I do."

I could have tried lying to him, but I was sure I couldn't fool him.

"My revolver is my revolver," I said.

He nodded. "Do you have money?"

"Maybe."

"How much?"

"Twenty."

"Twenty? For twenty bucks, Didi will give you a quickie, kid. One you won't forget."

"This pistol, it doesn't have to be anything special."

"For sure, you can depend on that." T.T. laughed, pulled his cigarettes out of his apron pocket and offered me the pack. I took one, and he lit it for me. Then he took one himself.

"A .38 would be enough," I said.

"You won't get one. Not for that price."

"How much?" I asked.

"Fifty."

"I don't have it."

"Nonsense. Everyone around here knows the price of a gun."

"I'm new at this."

"Then it's time for you to learn the prices. The price of a gun is fifty; it's all the same, whatever caliber and whatever brand."

"I don't have fifty. Word of honor."

"Word of honor?"

"Word of honor."

"How much do you have?"

"Thirty."

He looked at me doubtfully.

"Word of honor?"

"Yes."

"Show me."

I had everything ready, and I took a twenty and a ten out of my jeans pocket. He took both bills and looked at them carefully under the light of the bulb. In the bar, the jukebox began to play some ancient trucker song. Dave Dudley or someone I heard when I passed by the American bar at home.

"Wait here," he said, and he went out.

Didi came in. She looked at me strangely. As if he' had told her I'd only wanted to pay twenty dollars for the gun. She went to the refrigerator, opened it and quickly slammed it shut again.

"Damned pig's head," she snapped. "Startles me every time I open the fridge."

She came over and looked at me.

"I like you, little fella," she said. "You look like Anthony Quinn did when he was young."

I had no idea how Anthony Quinn looked when he was young. I hardly remembered I'd seen him once in a movie when he was about seventy. He looked like my great-grandfather, shortly before he died.

Didi began to pull out my shirt, and she was making eyes like a pig in love when, luckily, T.T. came back with a gun in the pocket of his apron.

He gave it to me, and I didn't have to look at it too closely. It was a shitty piece. A Saturday night special. Probably made of melted down scrap metal. Looked like a Colt, but it carried the name Kolt on the frame. It was a .38 caliber.

"New?" I asked.

"Hasn't even been fired yet," he said.

"Then how can you be sure it will fire?"

"It'll shoot, kid. Depend on it."

"I don't want to lose my customers."

He breathed in deeply. "I can't give you a guarantee. You get a guarantee buying detergent, not when you buy a gun. You have to trust me, dammit. I'm not a damned nigger, and I'm also not one of your redskin Indians from fuckin' Chiapas wherever the fuck that is."

It hurt my ears to listen to this guy speak.

"Then at least give me back the ten," I said.

He seemed to be considering. Then he said, "I'll give you five."

"Okay."

He gave me a five dollar bill, and I stuck the gun into my pants and left.

It was that simple. I was proud as a brightly colored rooster with a swollen comb. I, Santiago Molina, the king's new adjutant. I thought about making out with Nila in the bushes just to show her I was a man. She was always around, and Lucia wasn't. But when I got to where she was going to wait for me, she was not there. I called out for her several times, but I got no answer.

*

It was in all the newspapers on both sides of the border. A man who wanted to shoot his wife had the revolver explode in his hand. A piece of metal from the hammer went through his right eye and his skull and killed him on the spot. His wife, on the other hand, only suffered from shock, because her husband previously had not even hurt a fly.

One can only imagine that. Someone lives his entire life peacefully with his wife and then he suddenly cracks up. Poor wretch. Then he has even more bad luck and gets killed by an inferior handgun I had sold to him.

It was Monday morning when Flaco brought me the paper.

"A fellow killed himself with your gun," he said, and I thought first of suicide, naturally. It happens, again and again, someone has serious problems he can't cope with anymore and shoots a bullet into his mouth or into his ear. It even happened at home in our village.

"Read it to me," I said, yawning.

"I can't," he said

"You can't read?"

"I told you I can wipe my ass." He handed me the paper and distanced himself a bit, squatted on the edge of the canal and crapped in the bushes. When finished, he pulled up his pants without wiping his butt.

He sat down on the car seat somebody had dumped in the tunnel. "What does it say?" he asked me.

"Not much," I said without looking up from the newspaper. "It only says the man wanted to shoot his wife and got himself instead. The police assume that the pistol got smuggled across the border."

"Anything else?"

"It was a revolver. A .38 special."

I tossed him the newspaper. "At least wipe your ass," I said.

It was cold in the tunnel. Not far from me, Diego lay on his mattress. He lay there like a dead man, with his Walkman on his chest and his headphones around his throat. He had stolen the thing out of the trunk of a car. He was the best thief around, Flaco told me. Also, he had a sixth sense to smell through sheet metal all sorts of valuables in their hiding places, such as people locked in the trunks of their cars because the passenger cabin was too insecure.

"What's it look like outside?" I asked Flaco.

"Like always," he said. "The world turns."

Over the weekend, for half a million dollars, crack, cocaine, and marihuana slipped through a tunnel Bernardo controlled. As Diego told it, Flaco almost perished from having a fit. Choked or something. I wasn't there when it happened, but Nila talked to me about it. "He thinks the entire world is against him," she told me. "He talks himself into it. Bernardo always makes his own deals. He has good contacts in Hermosillo. But Flaco has had a persecution complex ever since Bernardo took over the other tunnel. It's gotten worse now, since Tomo."

Flaco and I left the tunnel. We went up to McDonald's, and each got a Big Mac meal. We went outside and sat on one of the stone benches under an umbrella. The border crossing wasn't even two hundred meters away from us, and we saw the pedestrians forming a long line, and the long line of cars on the main street.

"We will have to get rid of Bernardo," Flaco said suddenly, looking over to the border crossing.

"Why?"

"He takes too much business away from us."

"Do you have a plan for how you want to do this? Nila told me he always has a bunch of guys with him. Sometimes a dozen or so."

Flaco looked at me. "Do you know what I've been thinking?" he asked.

I shrugged.

"I' have been thinking that I made you my adjutant without actually knowing you."

I kept my silence.

"You carried off the deal with the revolver quite well, but this was just something I gave to you for a present."

"Because you don't have any credit left with T.T.," I said.

"I wouldn't have needed any credit for this deal. The man made a down payment to you, didn't he? I would have done the same with him."

"It wouldn't have mattered," I said

"Of course, it would have." His eyes were hard.

"T.T. doesn't want to do business with you until you pay him what you owe him."

"He'll get his money after we've done Bernardo. Then we'll do business again with the people in Hermosillo." He leaned over to me and put his grease-covered hand on my back. "If you want to show me what you're worth, put Bernardo away for us," he said.

"Shouldn't be a problem, Flaco."

I took a swallow of my Coke. He looked at me from the side with his mouth open. I took one of the cold, limp French fries from the bag, dunked it in a puddle of ketchup and stuck it into his mouth. He spit it over the wall, out into the street.

"No problem?"

"No problem."

"You'll do it?"

"Tell me where I can find him and I'll kill him for you."

"Simple as that?"

"Yes. You're the king, and I am your adjutant. That's the way it is, right? You want to know if you can trust me and what I'm worth. I don't think it's too much to demand from me."

"I'll show you the beginning and the end of his tunnel. It's the longer one of the two tunnels, but it's often used because it begins at the Red Cross station on the other side. The cops in their patrol cars seldom go by there."

He wanted to get up, but I said I wanted to finish my Big Mac first.

While we sat on the stone bench under the umbrella, dark storm clouds appeared over the hill behind the border crossing where the colorful little huts clung like toy houses.

Here in Nogales on this bright day, the sun still shone, and the sky directly over us was almost cloudless, but lightning flashed in the black clouds on the other side. Despite the traffic noise, I heard distant thunder.

"Rain is coming our way," I said with my mouth full.

"What?"

"Rain," I pointed over at the hill.

He nodded. "Hell," he said.

"What hell?" I asked.

"In the tunnels. If it's a bad storm, all hell will break loose. The tunnels were built to regulate the flood water, so the main canals don't overflow. Sometimes a canal is dry as a fart for months and then it changes in one minute into an underground torrent. Anyone who can't flee in time doesn't have a chance. I can tell you…"

He broke off because he noticed I was no longer listening. I saw Sombra go by on the other side of the street. She glanced over quickly, but she seemed not to see us.

As I jumped up, I told Flaco to wait for me there.

"Hey, hold on," he shouted after me, but I was already on the sidewalk and across the street. Sombra first noticed me when I was right behind her.

8
Sombra

"Oh, it's you," she said. "What was your name again?"

"Felipe," I said.

She laughed. "Are you chasing after me?"

"What if I was?"

She said nothing and looked me in the eye.

"Where are you going?" I asked.

"I'm on my way to school."

"Would it bother you if I walked along with you?"

"Not at all, but I don't think you want to encounter my mother."

"The teacher?"

"Yes."

"Why not?"

"Because she is a teacher, she would give you a lecture about life and why you should not go back into the tunnels."

"I might listen to her," I joked, knowing I shouldn't joke to her about my life.

She looked at me strangely. As if she had pity for me or something.

"Come," she said.

I looked around for Flaco, but he was no longer sitting on the bench under the umbrella. We went down the street together and through a side street to the school. It was a huge building. I had never seen a larger school before. Back in the village, the school was a small hut. This was three or four stories high, built of stone blocks with an impressive tile roof.

"Have you seen the girl with the cat again?" she asked me suddenly.

"Lucia?"

"You didn't tell me her name."

"The girl's name is Lucia."

"Have you seen her again?"

"No."

"I asked Bernardo to listen around among the polleros," she said.

"Bernardo?"

"Yes. Bernardo lives with friends in one of the tunnels. My mother once tried to guide him onto the right path, but all her efforts were in vain. Bernardo is a smart boy for all that. He can even read and write."

"I can too."

She didn't respond, and this irritated me because I wanted to prove to her that I could.

"What is so bad about living in the tunnels?" I said. "There's no place for us anywhere else. I can't go back to where I came from. I could never live there, where they killed my father and destroyed my family. In America, maybe you have a chance, we tell ourselves. So, I took the path to America."

"You're in America now."

"But illegally. The cops sitting over there in their patrol car would arrest me if they knew I'm here illegally."

"Believe me, they know. But it's too hot a day to deal with you. They sit in their patrol car with the air conditioning blowing on them. That one is Pete Arkin, and the other one is his partner, Javier Durazo. I know them well. They are too lazy to arrest a boy like you."

The cops looked over at us, and Sombra waved at them, and they grinned and waved back.

We went up to the school.

"The woman there on the steps is my mother," said Sombra.

I stopped walking.

"What's the matter?" she asked and turned to me.

"I'm leaving now," I said.

She smiled. "Will we see each other again?"

"Possibly," I said and shrugged my shoulders.

She looked at me thinking of something.

"Wait a moment," she said and ran over to her mother. When she came back, she had a slip of paper in her hand her mother had written a few numbers on.

"My telephone number," she said. "You can call anytime you want."

She gave me the paper, and I stuck it in my pants pocket.

"Adios," she said.

"Adios."

She ran back to her mother. I turned around and went back up the same street. The two cops watched me. I thought about waving to them like Sombra had, but I decided not to do something I might regret later. I walked back to the ditch that led to the concrete canal.

Flaco and Diego stood just in front of the tunnel entrance, looking up at the dark sky.

It was raining somewhere in the vicinity.

"What do you have to do with her?" Flaco asked me as I approached.

"Nothing," I said. "Why do you ask?"

"Because I don't trust her. Her father is with the Migra. Her mother is one of those who speak up for us. It doesn't fit together. And Sombra is on the loose."

"What's wrong about it?"

"I don't like it a bit. They claim she's not all there in the head because she doesn't know whether she's a girl or a boy."

"She's a girl," I said and left them both standing there.

*

143

Although it didn't rain, water flowed through the tunnels into the canal.

"The water comes from the hills," Flaco explained to me as we stood at the tunnel exit and looked at the foaming brown water and the large amount of trash it carried as it flowed into the canal. The water stank.

"Sometimes, when you stay too close to the water, your eyes start to get itchy," said Diego. "And if they get in contact with the water, it burns your eyeballs until you go blind."

I looked at the water flowing by us in disbelief.

"It's true," Flaco said. "It's full of industrious waste and battery acid and all kinds of poison."

Thunder from a distant storm rolled through the tunnel. Everyone was trying to find a higher place still dry. "It rained somewhere in the southern part of the city. The rainy season has begun."

It was late in July and the days were hot and sticky from the humidity and the torturous heat. In the morning, the skies were mostly cloudless, but toward midday the first white clouds would appear like the advanced guard of a fleet of battleships on their way to an epic battle. In the afternoon we could hear how they encountered each other and bombarded each other with their giant cannons, and we could see the flashing as they fired broadsides at the enemy ships and the sea of heavens became black from the smoke of burning battleships and the smoke of their cannons. We waited for one of these mighty battles to take place directly above us to watch it up close, but the real ones mostly took place in the distant horizon over the desert hills.

Once it rained on us, huge drops fell, dampening the earth and the dusty plants and the concrete and the asphalt. It smelled like it sometimes did at home. I left the city and went alone up a hill and as I came to the hilltop, I could see the battle going on over the southern horizon. A thousand bolts of lightning intertwined and the ships plowed into each other in the black smoke. A strong wind was blowing up here on the hilltop, and I made myself small and watched the battle. Then I looked down into a valley, and I saw some people crossing a ravine and running into a mesquite bosque on the other side, where they sought shelter from the storm.

I went down the hill, and it rained on my face. The people saw me coming, and a man came toward me. He had a shotgun in his hands, and he wore an old cowboy hat and a neckerchief, an armless undershirt and wet jeans. The man was a pollero. He pointed the shotgun at me.

"I was up there only by chance," I explained to him. "I saw you from there and—"

"What do you want?" he asked mistrustfully.

"I'm looking for a girl with a cat."

"There is no girl with a cat with us," he said. He pointed at the men, women, and children crouching under the mesquite trees, trying to protect themselves with their blankets. Fearful eyes stared at me.

"Has anyone seen a girl with a cat?" I called out to them.

A woman reached out her hand to me. "Come here, boy."

I went to her and crouched down by her. The woman was about thirty years old, maybe a little older.

"I saw a girl with a cat," she said.

My heart began to beat faster.

"Where?" I wanted to take her hand, but she pulled it back under her blanket.

"I saw a girl with a cat in Hermosillo," she said.

"A beautiful girl?" I asked quickly.

She smiled.

"Yes. I believe she was a beautiful girl."

"Where did you see her, Señora?"

"Where we slept there. In the backyard of a hotel."

"Did the girl say anything?"

"Yes. I asked her why she didn't come with us, and she explained to me she wanted to wait a few more days for someone."

"When was that?"

"Four days ago."

"Did she tell you her name, Señora?"

She shook her head.

"I'm sorry, but I don't know her name."

"Did she say anything else?"

"No."

"Are you sure?"

"I'm sorry, boy."

I stared into her eyes as if I could uncover Lucia's reflection in them. She must have seen Lucia with her dark, clear eyes containing no fear. I wished I could have seen in her eyes whether it was Lucia. Then I wouldn't have hesitated a moment to return to Hermosillo.

"I'm sorry, boy," she said once again.

"It's all right," I said and stood up. The man with the shotgun watched me. I told him I'd be going back to Nogales, so he let me pass, and he followed me out under the trees and into the rain. I stopped.

"We'll wait here until it's dark," he said. "After midnight, I'll bring them through one of the tunnels."

"How many are there?"

"Fifteen."

"Have you already paid for their passage?"

"No. I'll do it at the right time and right place."

"At the Hotel Camino Real?"

He nodded, and I left him standing in the rain and went along the streambed back into the city.

*

Nando died in the night.

Nila woke me up.

"Nando is dead," she said.

We carried him through the city and then we laid him down in a dark spot in the parking area of the Red Cross Station. A dog barked at us angrily from behind a fence of wire netting, and we hurried to get away from any people or the cops of Grupo Beta. Nila bent quickly over Nando and kissed him on his cold forehead; then she ran behind us back into the tunnel.

It rained through the night, and I couldn't sleep. I thought of Nando, and I hoped they'd found him in the meantime and had brought him in from the rain.

When I slept finally, I had a bad dream. I was home and my father came in through the door dragging a dead government soldier into the house and sat him on a chair at the table. "I found him outside," he told my mother.

"This man is dead," my mother screamed in fear. "Get him out of our house."

My father looked over to me. Then he handed me a gun. "Santiago, you kill him. It'll make you strong!"

I got up and got behind the chair and I noticed the hole in the back of the soldier's head. No blood, just a hole. When I pointed the gun at his neck, he turned his head and his face was nothing but a bloody mess.

I woke from that dream with cold sweat on my forehead and couldn't fall back asleep.

Toward morning, it stopped raining, and the air in the tunnel was damp and muggy. Nila came to me and wanted to sleep with me. I said I didn't have any urge to do so, and she got angry and spat in my face.

At sunrise, I left the tunnel. I bathed in the brackish red-brown water flowing down the canal. Today, the water didn't smell as bad. A few others came out of the tunnel and bathed. They approached me with care and respect, and nobody ventured into my vicinity. After I had bathed, I sat in the sun and thought of Nando. Then I thought of Lucia, and I became sad. I didn't particularly like this feeling, but my father had always told me it was part of life, the same as happiness and joy and all the rest. I didn't know whether my father was an unusually intelligent man or not, but he had a heart that determined his actions. That was what scared me most in my dream—that he was my father but at the same time he was a stranger to me.

"Nothing is lopsided if your heart has committed to something," he had once told me. My father had a heart. I had one to, not much different than his. After he got murdered, mine turned into a stone. And now, since I came in contact with Lucia, it was slowly becoming a heart again. I sensed it clearly. It was painful when I thought of Lucia. At the same time, I was filled with joy. I had no idea whether I would ever see her again, but even the fact she existed and was somewhere out there, made me feel like the happiest human in the world. I would have liked to tell my father this, but I didn't know how. So, I looked up at the sky for a sign, but there was nothing. No clouds. Nothing. I stood up, and I remembered I had promised Flaco I would kill Bernardo.

I called one of the boys to me.

"What's your name?" I asked him.

"Reynaldo," he said.

I placed my hand on his shoulder. It made him proud. "You know who I am, right?" I asked him.

"Yes." He nodded. "You are the new adjutant."

"Right." I slapped him on the shoulder. "Do you know Bernardo?"

"The one from the other tunnel or the one who hangs with José and me?"

"The one from the other tunnel, of course."

"I've seen him once in a while—"

"What do you know about him?"

"Nothing."

"Too bad."

I left him there and went through the tunnel, to get out on the other side. In America.

It was early in the morning. The air was clear. The sunlight crept slowly down the houses into the streets and alleys. A man stood at a public telephone by an automatic car wash and a coin laundry. I watched him, noticing him gesturing as he spoke. When he saw me he turned his back as if he was doing something secretive. I decided to wait until he had finished his talking. He went quickly by me, and when I could no longer see him, I went to the telephone and lifted the receiver. I dropped a quarter into the money slot and dialed the number Sombra had given me.

*

"It's me," I said.

"Ah. Felipe?"

"No. Not Felipe. Me."

"Didn't you tell me yesterday your name was Felipe?"

"You know what my name is."

She laughed. Then she said, "It certainly is a lovely morning, right?"

"Yes. I took a bath in the canal."

"You shouldn't do this."

149

"Why not?"

"Because the water is not okay."

"Why not?"

"Do you want to know exactly?"

"Yes."

"One moment. My mother will explain it to you."

"Wait, I—"

"Mom." I heard her call for her mother, and I broke out into a sweat and wanted to hang up and leave, but just then, the patrol car with the two cops I had seen the day before drove into the square in front of the laundry. They stopped and looked over. I dared not move from the spot.

"Hello, who is on the line?" a woman's voice asked me through the receiver.

"Ma—my name is Santiago," I stuttered.

"Then I know who you are. My daughter, Alexandra, told me about you."

"Alexandra?"

"Yes. That's our daughter's name. I know she gave you another name. Sombra, that's her fighting name. She believes herself to be a warrior fighting for justice."

"That—that is—"

She laughed. "Yes, I know what you want to say, Santiago. Justice is something that some can buy if they are rich enough. Alexandra said you came to us from Chiapas, and you want to get rich."

"I—this morning I washed in the canal," I said because I could not get rid of a sudden confusion in my head.

"You should not do this, Santiago. The water in the tunnels and the canals is poisonous. You should not come in contact with it, and you should never drink it."

I had seen some drink the water. The pictures ran through my head: children who drank the water; Nila drank it; a boy dipping water up with a bucket; the girl who washed her T-shirt.

"I haven't swallowed it," I said.

"The water is contaminated, Santiago," said Sombra's mother. "Full of dangerous bacteria. Shall I tell you the results of the latest tests from the health department?"

"Yes," I said, without having any idea why I said it.

"In one hundred milliliters of water, there was an e. coli bacteria count of two hundred twenty thousand. The acceptable limit for drinking water is at four thousand, Santiago."

I did not respond. I had never heard of such things before.

"You understand what I am trying to tell you, right?"

"Yes."

"The water is pure poison. Whoever drinks it can become seriously ill and, in the worst case, can even die."

I wanted to tell her that Nando had died last night, but I kept quiet because I wasn't sure whether the rape at the police station or some form of bacteria in the waste water had killed him.

"Most dangerous bacteria come from human and animal fecal matter," Sombra's mother continued. "Most of our wastewater comes from the hills, where some poor people still don't have functioning toilets or any other sanitary arrangements in their houses. And some is from the factories at the south end of town."

I kept quiet.

"Hello. Are you still there?"

I heard Sombra ask her mother for the receiver.

"Santiago?"

"Yes."

"What my mother wanted to tell you, really, is that some people crap in the ditches the wastewater runs through."

"Yes. That's what I understood."

"Good. So, it would be better if you did not bathe in it anymore. Maybe you could tell the others about the dangerous bacteria, I mean."

"I'm sure they would heed such warnings," I said with a faint smile.

She said nothing more. For a while, neither of us said anything more, but I heard her breathing, and I heard people talking in the background.

"Why did you call?"

"I don't know."

"You don't know why you called?"

"I wanted to talk with you."

"Ah. But you are not talking very much, Santiago. What's happening?"

"Nothing."

"You don't want to tell me? Are you in trouble?"

I could have told her I had rediscovered my heart and that I was confused because it hadn't turned out to be the stone I'd expected it to be. Nonetheless, I was ready to kill Bernardo. I didn't know how it was possible. I could have tried to explain everything, but I didn't. "No," I said instead.

"Do you want to meet with me?"

I wanted to tell her about the woman who had seen Lucia in Hermosillo. I wanted to tell her about Lucia; that she came from Guatemala. I wanted to describe Lucia's face; this beautiful face in which nothing fit but everything went well together as if a master artist had created her.

"Santiago?"

I hung up, crossed the plaza near the car wash and went down to the canal. I asked a boy about Bernardo. He pointed to the opening of a large concrete tunnel under a street overpass. A police car was parked up there.

"There," he said.

After the patrol car had left, I went down the ditch to the tunnel. Before I got there, I reached for the revolver in my belt and pulled it out a bit so I could get it into my hand quicker.

*

"Bernardo?" I asked the guy. He sat on the Mexican side of the tunnel on a junk motorcycle. Behind him, on the back fender, sat a girl in a black dress. It was so short, it didn't cover a single centimeter of her legs. On top, it was cut very deeply.

This girl almost struck me blind. She had wild black hair and dark red lips, and she wore mirror-lensed sunglasses and large golden earrings.

"What do you want from me?" the guy asked. He also wore shades, and I couldn't see his eyes behind the dark glasses.

"I heard a group of pollos is coming through your tunnel tonight," I said. "Some of them women and children."

He took a pack of cigarettes out of the breast pocket of his shirt, which hung over his pants. He opened it, pulled out one of the cigarettes with his lips and the girl lit it with a golden cigarette lighter.

He blew smoke at me.

"Who are you?"

"Santiago," I said. "A friend of Sombra's."

He stroked the girl's thigh as he looked at me.

"What do you think of my girl?" he asked.

I shrugged my shoulders.

He laughed. "Someone told me Flaco got himself a new adjutant whose name is Santiago."

I reached for my revolver. It could not escape Bernardo watchful eyes.

"That's you, right?"

"I've come here to ask you a favor," I said.

"What can I do for you, my friend?"

"I am looking for a girl with a cat."

The girl laughed sardonically.

"What's so damn funny?" he said.

"He's looking for a girl with a pussy," the girl said, and she laughed at her joke. "Bernardo, he said—"

"I know what he said. Leave."

The girl got off and tugged at her dress, but it simply did not want to fit right.

"Get lost!" he ordered her coldly.

The girl's eyes flashed. I thought she was going to hit him, but she turned around and left, her hips swinging.

She had beautiful slender legs, and she wore shoes with extremely high heels. She didn't look back even once as she left, but she almost fell when one of her feet turned.

"Who's the girl?" he asked me. "The girl with the cat."

"A girl I met while traveling and then we somehow lost each other."

"And now you are waiting for her here?"

"Yes."

"It's nearly impossible to find a chick with a cat. Maybe the chick got separated from the cat in the meantime?"

"She would never get separated from her cat."

He looked at me as if he doubted my ability to understand what he tried to tell me.

"But it is possible the cat strayed away from her."

"Strayed? I don't think that cat—"

"Run off or something. Run over by a car. Dammit, what do I know what can happen to a pussy?" He looked for the girl with the short dress, but she had already disappeared.

I could have killed him then. There was nobody nearby. I

quickly looked around again, looked into the tunnel and up the canal to the place where it made a turn and where the girl had disappeared.

"What is it?" he said. "What are you afraid of? That Flaco will suddenly appear and see you here with me?"

"No."

"You are deceiving him, my friend."

"I'm not doing that."

"He certainly would not like to see you here with me."

"I only want to ask you to tell me if the girl goes through your tunnel."

"This is not that easy," he said. "Where would I find you? In one of Flaco's tunnels? I can't go there. They would kill me."

"Not if you tell them I'm expecting you."

He took off his sunglasses and looked at me, squinting.

"You told me you're a friend of Sombra's."

"That's right."

"I could get a message to Sombra, and she could get it on to you."

"This would also be possible," I said. "I just don't want a girl to get held up in the tunnel."

"The girl means a lot to you, right?"

"Yes."

He stretched out his arm and pointed to my stomach.

"You have a gun hidden under your shirt, right? Show it to me."

I pulled it out from under my shirt and showed it to him. He looked at it a while and nodded in acknowledgment.

"Good," he said. "I'll give you a shout if the girl with the cat shows up in our tunnel."

Without waiting for an answer, he started his motorcycle and rode away through the canal. I stuck the gun back in the waist of my pants and walked through Nogales, Sonora. I was convinced I only needed to walk around, and I would come across Lucia somewhere. I walked around all day. Late in the afternoon, I stood before the Hotel Camino Real. I went in through the front entrance. Behind the reception desk, dressed in black, there was Sarita. She was reading a newspaper.

As I entered, she looked up and met my eyes over her glasses.

"Where do I know you from?" she asked.

"I was here last week. At night."

She laid the newspaper on the desk. "Yes, now I remember. What was your name?"

"Santiago."

My glance fell onto the newspaper and a photo showing Don Fernando. He lay on the veranda of his hacienda, on the painted tiles, and I recognized him even though I could see only a part of his face. It was turned to the side, and blood ran out of his mouth. Some men stood around him, and on the right edge of the picture, there was a piece of a white dress and a leg and foot without a shoe. The leg belonged to Carmelita. I could tell immediately.

I stared at the newspaper, and it felt as if my heart wanted to jump out of my chest. I could not breathe, and I could not move. I just stood there, and the photo in the newspaper began to dance.

"What's with you, boy?" I heard the dark voice of the woman ask. "Are you ill?"

I wanted to tell her I knew the man who was lying there and bleeding on the tiles, but no sound came from my lips.

Then she took the newspaper and pointed at the photo. "A horrifying bloodbath," she said. "Apparently some killers of a drug cartel murdered this brave man and his family. They killed even his bodyguard and several horses."

I had to hold onto the edge of the desk. My knees were so weak I would have collapsed if I hadn't had something to steady myself.

*

The storm unloaded itself directly over the city. It was so dark outside it seemed to be night in the afternoon. Everyone fled the tunnels, taking a few valuable belongings. Some of them hung out at the railroad tracks looking for shelter under loading ramps and in metal sheds used for storage, others just disappeared into the city.

Flaco and I entered a tavern that had only a wooden counter and five or six abused barstools. Flaco knew the man who owned the tavern. His name was Manny. The place was called Manny's Bar. Like with T.T. with his saloon on the other side of the street, they both had to be very creative people. The only difference, at T.T.'s, pictures of baseball players hung on the wall behind the counter. At Manny's, yellowed black and white photographs of movie stars were pinned to the wall. Someone had burned a hole in Marilyn Monroe's bottom with a cigarette. Other decorations in Manny's Bar I noticed were a wreath of plastic flowers, which came from a grave, and a horse skull painted green.

We each drank a beer and Flaco passed around his flask of mescal. The men at the bar talked about women. Thunder shook the little bar. The glasses rattled on the shelves. The street outside was a stream.

"That guy who wanted to shoot his wife had damned bad luck," one of them said.

"He must have been a rank beginner," another said laughing.

"As if someone could practice killing his wife, man. Nobody

kills more than one wife in his lifetime, I guess. With a crappy handgun, you might fail on your first try."

"He should have bought a real Colt. What happened to him would have never happened to him with a real Colt."

They weren't drunk, but they drank a lot and they talked a lot without saying much. It amused me how important some of their topics seemed to them.

Flaco and I drank another beer.

The storm gradually let up.

"Damned little storm," said one of the men. "Lasted only a few minutes."

"Short as Manny's prick," said another. They laughed and slapped each other on the backs. I hated them. Don Fernando had died for these kinds of wretches. So they could go full bore in Manny's Bar and laugh over their stupid jokes. I reached for my revolver. Flaco saw it in my eyes first, and then he saw my hand disappear under my shirt.

"Qué mierda!" he whispered. "Come on, let's get out of here."

Flaco had me pay. He knew I still had money from selling the gun. Before we were too drunk to walk, we left Manny's Bar and went to where I had seen Flaco for the first time and where the old woman lived. With a blank expression on her face, she sat in front of a small black-and-white TV. An old Hollywood film was playing, with Charlton Heston and Gregory Peck, who were arguing with each other in Spanish and ended up beating each other until they could no longer stand.

Flaco asked the old woman about a girl named Rita. She said Rita had not been here. Then Flaco kicked at the chair she was sitting on.

"Are you drunk, Flaco?" she asked him while Charlton Heston and Gregory Peck beat each other up. "You shouldn't drink that much, do you hear? Or you'll end up just like your father."

We went out, and Flaco called this Rita up from a public telephone. He told her he wanted to sleep with her, and me with her friend, and explained where they should meet us.

We waited in the park for them. The flask was nearly empty when they arrived. I was no longer level-headed. Everything seemed mixed up. Up was down and left was right.

Flaco wanted to explain clearly to the girls what had happened.

"Some kind of bastards massacred his entire family," he babbled while he reached under Rita's dress with both hands. "It's in the paper."

"Who is he?" Rita asked, gesturing at me.

"My adjutant." Flaco took the girl to another park bench and pulled the slip from her legs. I sat and stared at the girl standing in front of me.

"Come," she whispered while she bent over me and pushed her breasts into my face. "What's your name?" she whispered.

"San—" I had to catch my breath.

"San? And what else?"

"Santiago."

The girl was fumbling around with the fly on my pants. Flaco was lying on top of Rita, and the white slip lay on the ground. I grabbed the girl, whose name I did not know, by the throat and squeezed till she fell to her knees. I kept strangling her, and she wheezed and opened her mouth wide.

I threw myself off the park bench and ran away. I ran down to the canal and saw that it was full of water. I asked a boy who sat shivering under a plastic tablecloth about Bernardo, but the boy didn't know anything about him. I climbed the hill to where the iron wall stopped, and the barbed wire fence began. I crawled through a hole in the fence over the border and went back down the hill to Nogales, Arizona.

From behind a small wall near the carwash, I saw a couple of kids fall upon a boy and beat him until he didn't move anymore. The cops and an ambulance came, but the cops looked around only briefly and asked a man from the nearby gas station what had happened. The man told them nothing unusual had happened. "It's been going on like this for months. Nothing and nobody is secure anymore in the presence of those rats in the tunnels." He showed the cops his gun, which he carried in a holster. "I keep them away from me with this," he said, "for dead sure." The cops laughed, climbed into their patrol car and drove away.

To sleep, I went to a gutted-out wrecked car where I had already spent a night. Before I crawled in, I beat against the dented metal of the hood to drive out the snakes and other vermin. But as I forced open the back door, I noticed a thick rattlesnake coiled up on the seat, and it rattled at me. I took the piece of iron from the ground and threw it at the snake and only hit the open door. The snake glided from the seat, and I waited until it was out. When I saw it in the starlight between the pieces of junk lying on the ground, I grabbed a piece of concrete and killed it.

I crawled into the car and slept. Sometime in the night, I awoke from a nightmare I could not remember. Bathed in sweat. I left the car, went down to the canal and lay on the embankment, so my legs hung into the water. I stayed there until dawn. When I got up, I noticed a young lifeless coyote near my left leg. He was probably surprised by the water in one of the tunnels and drowned. I pushed him away from me. Half covered by foam, he floated down the canal in the brownish water surrounded by trash.

*

I went to the school. There, I sat down in the shade of a tree and watched how the small children ran around on the playground.

I tried to think of Lucia, but without success. I thought of Don Fernando and Señor Silva and, above all, of Carmelita. They had all been killed, including old Pedro, who had hidden in the horse barn. In the newspaper it had said a helicopter with masked men landed in the plaza in front of the hacienda. First, they killed Señor Silva in the watchtower and then they forced their way into the house and herded everyone there into Don Fernando's study. They tied everyone's hands behind their backs. Don Fernando's son Antonio tried to defend himself, and they shot him down with a burst from a submachine gun in his father's study. Don Fernando's daughter Luisa was raped before they killed her. And Don Fernando and Carmelita, for reasons yet unknown, died together on the veranda. No one knew who was responsible for the massacre. Probably the drug mafia, according to the paper. Because Don Fernando would not allow them to bribe him. The federal judge and his family were now martyrs for justice. Mexico was a just land. A paradise. A land of honorable women and men who would not lend themselves to corruption.

It was all a bunch of nonsense, but I knew that newspaper had to write such things to please the politicians and keep the truth from people.

I did not see Sombra coming. I did not hear her. She was a shadow united with mine. Suddenly, she was sitting next to me under the tree.

"I've been looking for you," she said. "Why are you crying?"

I hadn't been aware I was shedding tears. I turned away from her and my chest burned. I wept while I tried not to and

161

I almost choked. She let me cry. She sat next to me and did not move. She did not say a word.

When I finally got a grip on myself again, I wiped my face.

"Have you already had breakfast?" she asked.

"No."

"Okay, let's go to McDonald's."

So that's what we did. I told Sombra about Don Fernando and his family. I told her the revolver I'd hidden under my shirt had belonged to Pedro. She heard me through without interrupting. When I had told her everything there was to tell, we left McDonald's and strolled down the street and up a grassy hill where scattered trees grew.

We lay down in the grass and watched the clouds and didn't say a word to each other until she told me it was her birthday and her mother had invited a few people to dinner that evening. "It's nothing special," she said. "But it would please me very much if you would come too, Santiago."

The truth was I wanted to watch for Lucia that evening, because I had started sensing she might be close that morning. I was sure she was there, somewhere in Nogales, hidden with others waiting for the night and the coyotes.

Sombra got up and distanced herself a few steps. She looked over the scene along the way, which showed Nogales spread out and divided in the middle by a wall of iron.

"If you don't want to come I'll understand," she said without looking at me.

"It's not that I don't want to come," I said.

She turned around and looked at me. "What is it then, Santiago?"

I got up quietly and turned away from her.

There were many hills spreading out to the north. Hills and hollows and narrow valleys, covered with gold-yellow grass reaching to my waist. I touched the blades and they bent softly under my hands. The sun disappeared behind a dark cloud. We stood in its shadow, and we watched the other shadows gliding over the hollows and valleys like beings from a place where there was no sound.

"I am sixteen today," Sombra said suddenly. "Seventeen years ago, this was a different world, I believe."

"It must have been another world," I said. "In seventeen years it would have been impossible for the world I knew to turn into the world I know today."

"Seventeen years—that's not much time in a world tens of thousands of years old."

"Tens of thousands?"

"Millions."

She came to me and took me by the hand. We walked over the crest of the hill and along a fence to a path that led west—a path nothing more than two wheel ruts. The puddles that remained from the rain of the previous day mirrored the sky and the clouds.

We followed the path to the main road. A run over dog lay there. A man sat on the embankment at the edge of the road, drinking coffee out of a thermos. His dark face glistened with sweat. He watched us. As we went by him, he asked us what time it was.

"It's ten after three," said Sombra. The man was waiting for someone. For a car that would take him home from work before it began to rain again.

9
Lucia

There was scarcely any water left in the tunnels from yesterday's storm, but no one dared move back in for the night.

"This will be a night for the smugglers," Flaco said to me as we went through the main tunnel. "They didn't come through yesterday and the risk was also rather high the day before. But tonight it won't rain."

He was right. The sky was clear and starry, and the waxing moon was a sharp sickle.

"Will anyone come through our tunnel?"

"Cocaine from Colombia," he said.

"No illegals?"

"Oh, yes. Two large groups. There's a chicken among them."

"How do you know?"

"Got it from Sarita. She tells me every time there is one."

"And who will pluck this chicken?"

"Diego and a couple of other guys. They will wait at the end of the tunnel near the bridge. The man is alone. Sarita has already taken part of his money, and he has paid the coyotes. At the tunnel entrance, I will ask him if he wants to pay a special tax for his passage. It would guarantee a pollero brings him safely through the tunnel. If he is smart, he will give me a hundred bucks. But most of them are as dumb as a chicken, and stingy."

"If he pays you a hundred dollars, will he get through?"

"All the way to the other side."

"And on the other side?"

"Diego and the others will take delivery of him."

"To rip him off once more? Or even kill him for all his money?"

"Only if it's necessary. Whatever Diego and his boys take

from him gets divided among us all? Only the hundred bucks are for me alone."

I said nothing more. We were strolling down the street leading to the Hotel Camino Real, but we went past the hotel entrance. Flaco asked me why I almost strangled the girl on the park bench. I had almost forgotten.

"Tell me, has anybody ever said you might not have all your marbles, my friend?" he asked.

I didn't answer.

"Do you sometimes hear voices, maybe?"

"Voices of whom?"

"The voices of your Maya ancestors?" he insisted. "Or in your head, do you see strange pictures sometimes?"

"I see the old gringo, Papa Biddle."

"Who is he?"

"The Santa Claus who got under my sister's skirt."

He stopped and bent over laughing. I turned away so he couldn't see into my eyes. They would have given me away.

"Tell me about Papa Biddle," he demanded.

I didn't tell him anything. We crossed the canal and went up the street to Manny's Bar.

"I'll buy you a beer," said Flaco.

There were no customers in the bar. Manny sat in front of a small TV set. He was wearing a dirty blue undershirt and shorts. A ventilator was running in the ceiling. Marilyn laughed at us seductively from her poster; she winked at me. The picture on the TV was no bigger than a postcard. It was snowy, but Manny said it was only static because lightning had probably struck somewhere.

"You should buy a new TV," Flaco suggested. "They say pretty soon there will be color TV."

"Can you even imagine that?" said Manny. "Hell, I can't even get a good picture in black and white."

We drank a beer. The ventilator cooled my head a little and dried the sweat on my face.

"They caught one of the people who killed the judge and his family," said Manny. "He's the son of a high government official, but they don't want to tell us who it is yet."

"The son of the president, perhaps," said Flaco.

I said nothing. I learned to despise the president of Mexico. My father held him responsible for what happened in Chiapas during his reign—for the killing of thousands of our people, many of the women and children.

"Does he even have a son?" asked Manny while staring at his little TV. Football was on. Excerpts from the game between Cruz Azul and Atlante.

"I'm going now," I said and placed a dollar bill on the counter.

"What's that for? A dollar? I invited you, my friend."

I went to the door without telling him why I wanted to get rid of the dollar bill, despite the fact that the one Biddle had given me, was not in my possession anymore. He probably wouldn't have understood the shame I carried.

"Buy yourself a cigar," I said and opened the door.

"Where are you going?" Flaco asked through a cloud of smoke.

On the TV, Atlante's goalkeeper stopped a penalty kick.

"Felix is the man!" roared Manny. "He has to play on the national team and not this other dude—what's his name anyway…"

I didn't want to hear about our national team, so I went out. It was humid and hot outside, even though it was dark. In the light of the streetlamps, millions of moths fluttered.

I went down to the Hotel Camino Real. The same man met me in the hallway who had met me the first time. He was naked above the waist. Sweat glistened on his hairy chest.

"Fuck, what do you want here?"

"I'm looking for a girl with a cat."

"Go away, punk."

I had just decided to kill him when Sarita came down the stairs. "Juan, this kid is Flaco's adjutant," she warned.

He should have kissed her feet, because she had just saved his life. But he just grinned and disappeared behind the staircase like a dog with no bark.

"What is it, Santiago?" said Sarita.

"I'm looking for the girl with the cat."

"Do you know she's here?"

"Yes."

She took me around back. Behind the hotel was a small courtyard enclosed by a high wall. In this courtyard, there were more than two dozen people—women, children and men, some standing and some sitting on the ground.

"Miguel, this boy here is looking for a girl with a cat," Sarita said to a man who was leaning against the wall by the gate, smoking a cigarillo. The man was small and angular. He had muscular arms with hands much too large for the rest of him.

"A girl with a cat?" he asked through a cloud of blue smoke. "Have a look around, boy."

I looked around quickly. If Lucia were among these people, I would have recognized her immediately.

"These here, they will go through Flaco's tunnel," said Sarita.

I looked at the men, trying to recognize the chicken among them. But I could not have said with certainty which one was him. They all looked run down, but none had the sign of impending death. I never knew what this sign was when my grandmother talked about it.

"That one there, Santiago. He is marked for death," she used to tell me, pointing at a man standing in the street, sitting on a bench in the plaza, kneeling in church. I had no idea what she saw, but I was sure she could have pointed out the man if she'd been here.

Sarita led me back to the hotel where Juan stood in a doorway in the dark. Only his eyes glowed and revealed him. They didn't tell me his thoughts, but they revealed him just the same.

"If he crosses me one more time, I will kill him, Señora," I said to Sarita, who was standing behind me.

"He is my lover," she whispered. "Don't kill him until I've had enough of him."

*

I telephoned Sombra.

"Where do you live?" I asked.

"You would never find it," she said. "Tell me where you're calling from and I'll pick you up. I just got my driver's license."

"From the car wash," I said. "From a public telephone."

"Wait for me there."

She hung up, and twenty minutes later, a Subaru station wagon drove into the parking lot. Behind the steering wheel sat Sombra. She stopped, turned off the engine and climbed out.

"Santiago," she called.

I did not move.

She turned around once and then she started toward the gas station to ask about me there. I stepped out of the shadow of a dumpster.

"Santiago, I thought you'd taken off," she said. "Come on, get in. Dinner's already on the table."

We drove through the city. Although she had just gotten her driver's license that day, her sixteenth birthday, she handled the car as if she had come into the world in an old Subaru.

I wasn't sure what to do with my gun. As a Migra officer, her father was trained to detect a concealed weapon on a guy like me. I took it out of the waistband of my pants. "Where should I put this?" I asked her. "I probably shouldn't take it into the house."

"Probably not," she said. "Put it under your seat."

She didn't say anything else about it. At the outskirts of the city, she stopped in front of a small house in a row of other small houses. Bright lights illuminated the rooms. From the other houses came only light from television sets. Air conditioners on the roofs hummed. I realized that most people heard nothing but such noises their entire lives. There was room for nothing else in their heads but these noises that drowned everything else out.

Sombra went into the house before me. It was ice-cold inside. I was startled when I saw her father. He wore a starched and ironed uniform and his gold badge flashed. I had almost forgotten he worked for the Migra.

"Papa, I asked you to put on a different shirt," Sombra complained.

His face was without expression. Like stone. He didn't offer me his hand.

"I can't exactly say I'm happy about your visit, boy," he said. "Alexandra has already told us quite a lot about you."

"There is not all that much to say about Santiago," said Sombra's mother, laughing as she took her husband's arm. "Could you, perhaps, forget for a little while that you work for the Migra?"

He withdrew his arm from her. "Let's sit down," he said, and he went to the table, which was extravagantly set and colorfully decorated.

"He likes you, but he doesn't want to show it," Sombra

murmured to me. "A conflict of conscience, I guess?"

Eight of us sat at the table in the dining room. All except for me were relatives of Sombra's. An uncle from Chicago, who wore a hearing aid. An aunt with two little girls. Her husband was in Europe for the military. In Germany. She told us of a trip to Germany and how gray everything was there and how it had rained the whole time they were there. "We almost grew gills," she said. "Right, girls?"

"Yes!" they both cried. Then one of them said, "The carrots, I don't want to eat them."

"Then leave them on the plate, sweetheart," said Sombra's mother. "I didn't like carrots either when I was young."

I sat beside Sombra. The chair on the other side of me was empty. None of them had any idea how much I wished Lucia would come in and sit in that chair. The meal was excellent, but I froze from the air conditioning. I emptied my plate. It had been an eternity since I'd eaten that well. Tamales and everything. Tasty beans. Sweet potatoes, crisp tacos. Enchiladas and burritos. It smelled almost like at home. I thought about my mother and when we were still a family.

"Where do you come from, Santiago?" the uncle from Chicago asked me.

"Chiapas," I said.

"Huh?" He bent far across the table and screwed up his face.

"Chiapas," I said a bit louder.

He fumbled around with his hearing aid.

"Santiago comes from Chiapas," the aunt shouted in his ear.

"Chiapas?" he asked.

"Yes."

"Ah, Chiapas, huh?"

Half of his burrito fell onto his pants. Sombra laughed, and her mother took a paper napkin and wiped him off.

For dessert, there was flan. I ate two bowlfuls because the uncle hated caramel pudding. Sombra's mother turned on a CD player. "Simon and Garfunkel," said Sombra. "'Bridge over Troubled Water' is my mother's favorite song. I like it all—"

"In Chiapas, people are beating each other's heads in," the uncle shouted suddenly. "Indians or whoever."

"No longer," said Sombra's father. "It's been quiet down there for several months now."

"The quiet before a storm," said the aunt.

"Are you an Indian?" the uncle asked me. "You look like an Indian. A Maya or something."

"I am a Tzotzil," I said.

"A what?"

"A Tzotzil," I shouted in the uncle's ear.

"They're descendent from the Mayas," explained Sombra's father without looking at me. "Once a highly civilized people."

They talked about Chiapas and the Zapatista Rebellion. Although they wanted me to feel welcome in their house, I still felt like an outsider. It was of no concern to me what they said about Chiapas, because they had no idea what was happening there. Only Sombra's mother had a clue. She said that nearly 12,000 indigenous people were killed in this rebellion. She called it genocide. Sombra's father looked at me. I said nothing.

Everyone seemed to have a good time, but the gaiety of the women and the two girls did not move me. Sombra noticed. She put her hand on my arm and smiled.

After we had finished eating, I went with her outside in front of the house. The high humidity made the air sticky. There was no breeze. Lightning flashed over the city and the hills to the southeast. Thunder rolled softly through the night.

The two girls came out and hopped around noisily on the

front lawn for a minute or so until they noticed how muggy it was outside.

The uncle sat back in a chair on the veranda. Sombra's father smoked a cigarette. Her mother and aunt were in the kitchen, filling the dishwasher.

Again the uncle asked me where I was from.

"Chiapas," I said.

"Where?"

"Chiapas."

"He's gotten forgetful in his old age," said Sombra. "And hard of hearing."

"From the noises," I said

"From what noises?"

"You don't hear them?"

"No, I don't hear anything."

I told her I had to go back.

"To where?"

"To the tunnels."

I excused myself and said goodbye to everyone. Except to Sombra's father. He was, by chance, in the bathroom.

On the way into the city, I told Sombra that Lucia would be coming through a tunnel tonight.

"How do you know?" she asked.

"I don't, but I sense that she's nearby."

Sombra looked at me. "Do you love this girl?"

"I don't know," I answered, and it was the truth. "I'm not sure what love is."

She parked by the car wash.

"Don't forget your gun," she reminded me. I took it from under the seat and shoved it into my pants. She watched me trying to place the gun so it wouldn't bother me.

"Okay," I said when I was done. "It felt good to be with you and your family. And thanks for the ride."

"I'm going with you," she said.

I stared at her, speechless.

"I'm going with you," she said again. She opened the door and stepped out of the car.

*

It was still early. The immigrants would not be making their way to the tunnels before midnight. The cops on both sides were patrolling the streets. Sometimes, they would stop at the edge of the canals and illuminate the tunnel entrances with their spotlights, but they did not dare to climb down into the canals, much less enter. Many of the Mexican cops were corrupt and collected bribe money, and the gringo cops held back because they knew very well we would stop them, maybe even shoot at them, if they crossed us in the tunnels.

A little past eleven we ran into Nila on the Mexican side. She was with Diego, but he was in a hurry to get away.

"What are you doing here?" said Nila to Sombra. "I thought you were Bernardo's girl."

"I'm nobody's friend," Sombra said.

"She is my friend," I said quickly.

"Flaco will certainly be happy about that," snapped Nila turning around to leave, but I held her back by the arm.

"Wait. I got to tell you something."

She pulled her arm away and looked at me with burning eyes.

"The girl is coming through one of the tunnels today."

"What girl?"

"I already told you about her. The one with the cat."

Nila nodded toward Sombra. "And what about her?"

"Four eyes see more than two. We don't know which group the girl is with. We also don't know which tunnel—"

"What could you know when you don't know anything?" Nila interrupted.

"He knows she's near. That's enough, okay?" said Sombra and her voice sounded different, hoarse. Nobody hearing her would have known she wasn't a boy.

They stared at each other. I sensed the tension between them.

Nila turned to me. "What's your girl's name again?"

"Lucia."

"Why don't you ask the polleros at the Red Cross?"

"We're just about to go there," said Sombra.

Nila shook her head. "We should separate. Until midnight, practically nobody tries to sneak through the tunnels. While we ask the polleros at the church about the girl, you go to the Red Cross station, Santiago. There's a group of immigrants gathering there. They'll be taken through Bernardo's tunnel. But be careful not to make the drug smugglers nervous with your asking around about the girl. That could be dangerous."

"Don't worry. Do you know where Flaco is?"

"Collecting money."

Nila walked away, stopped after a few steps and turned her head toward us.

"Are you coming or not? Four eyes see more than two."

"And six still more," Sombra answered. She hesitated a moment, then she went with Nila.

*

A strong wind blew through the streets of Nogales, from the southeast to the northwest, crossing the border, which meant nothing to it. It tore at the few trees in the park as if trying to uproot them. It lifted corrugated iron sheets from a storage shed near the freight depot, were a group of desperate people waited for the guide who would lead them through the tunnel.

The stoplights swung back and forth on their cables. Tiles fell from roofs. People sought shelter, hurrying through the streets and disappearing into narrow alleys. Traffic was sparse on the main street. The small tourist shops had closed, and the begging Indian women had fled with their children.

In the distance, lightning flashed, followed by low thunder. In the light of a street lamp, I looked down into the canal. Only a small stream branched between islands of trash and debris.

I looked up at the sky and was struck by the clarity of each individual star.

Near the Red Cross station, I saw a man who was trying to light a cigarette, and I asked him about Lucia. He pointed to a building where someone had painted the face of Che Guevara. There, in red letters: VIVA LA REVOLUCIÓN. It looked as if blood was dripping from each letter, glittering like rubies.

I approached the door, and a dim light shone through the window. After I knocked, Bernardo pulled open the door. He was smoking a cigar, and he grinned when he recognized me, looking like a businessman who had just made some serious money.

"Hey," he said. "I wasn't expecting you."

He let me enter. People stood around in a large room. Some sat on the floor, leaning against the wall. It didn't look any different than the back courtyard of the hotel, where they waited for polleros. Mistrustful and curious eyes of women and children. Fearful and threatening eyes of men who stood with their backs to the wall and felt responsible for everything.

Lucia saw me before I saw her.

She sat on the floor with her cat in her lap. A woman

rested her head against Lucia's shoulder. The woman looked exhausted and scared. She was nursing a baby. She avoided my gaze by lowering her head.

Lucia whispered to the young mother who sat up for Lucia. No one said a word, but they all watched us. Lucia came to me, and my heart thumped madly in my chest and my knees shook. She passed me to go outside. Bernardo asked her through the cigar smoke if she was coming back. She looked at him briefly and nodded.

*

We crouched behind a wall to avoid the wind, and I told her I had been waiting for her.

"You waited for me?" she asked in disbelief.

"I knew you would come here one day on your way to America."

She was silent.

"I told everybody to watch out for you. Bernardo, too."

"Is Bernardo the boy these people paid for passage through his tunnel? The one with the fat cigar?"

"Yes, but you shouldn't have payed. I'll take you along through my tunnel."

"You have a tunnel of your own?" she asked almost sarcastically.

"Well, it isn't really my tunnel. It's Flaco's tunnel."

"Who's Flaco?"

"The king," I said proudly.

"The king?"

"Yes."

"And his kingdom?"

"What do you mean by that?"

"Every king has a kingdom, Santiago."

"Flaco's kingdom is one of the tunnels leading across the border."

"That's his kingdom? A tunnel?"

"Yes. And I am Flaco's adjutant."

She looked at me. Even though it was dark behind the wall, I saw the light in her eyes.

"That's a sinister kingdom, Santiago," she said. "I don't think you should be so proud of being Flaco's adjutant."

I lowered my head. I did not like the tone of her voice.

"It's better to be a king or his adjutant than some beggar. No matter what kingdom you're in."

She did not respond.

"Don't you think so?"

"Why are you asking me?"

"Who else can I ask?"

"You know." She laughed. "Ask the cat."

"How would she know the right answer? She has never been in the tunnels before."

"That's true. She might not even be alive anymore."

"I'm alive."

"Others aren't."

"I live well."

"Because you've been lucky until now."

I grinned. "Whoever wants to get to the top needs a whole lot of luck."

"Is that your goal? To stay here and become a king like Flaco?"

I felt defiance rise in me. Lucia was asking me to defend myself, but I didn't know how. I had expected our reunion to be different.

"What do you know about Flaco and me and the tunnels?" I said. "You just got here."

"No. I've been here since yesterday. I've listened around. I know that this Flaco is just a small-time crook and not a kingpin. He and his friends live in the tunnels and are paid by smugglers. Also, they rob people, and now and then, they even murder them. That is—"

I grabbed her by the arm and held it tightly.

"You cannot insult me," I said, my voice shaking.

She turned her head. "Let me go!"

"Do you hear? You can't insult me."

"I don't want to. Why would I want to? You are who you are, and I am who I am. We'll probably never meet again."

She pulled her arm away. I reached out for her arm again, but this time, she defended herself. At that, I lost control. I grabbed her hair with my other hand and tried to pull her to me, but before I had her arm locked, she drove her knee into my groin. I doubled over with pain and fell to my knees. I fell to the ground and writhed like a worm on the asphalt; my fists pressed into my lower body. I could not get air, and it felt as if my head would collapse. I even lost consciousness for a few minutes. When I woke, the pain had dulled, but I still felt a hellish burning. I saw Lucia standing on the wall. The wind tore at her dress and her hair. She looked down at me as if I were a dog she just had kicked.

I tried to get on my feet, but the pain did not let me.

"Why... did you...do that?" I asked between breaths.

"Don't bother me again!" she said.

"I... I didn't want to do anything to you," I answered carefully while I raised myself with one hand. The pain in my groin brought tears to my eyes. "Where... where did you learn that?"

"From my mother. She was a comandante with the rebels, and she convinced me to fight with her against the soldiers."

I stared at her. She laughed suddenly and came up to me. She stopped close to me. She wore ankle-high boots and a dress reaching down to her knees. She had strong legs.

"I have never felt such pain before," I coughed.

"Don't be a sissy, Santiago. Someone who wants to be king in the tunnels has to be tough, even merciless, when enduring pain."

"What do you know of pain, dammit."

"A bit," she said, and she raised her skirt and showed me a scar that began at her hip and led to the knee. Even in the weak light falling over the wall, I could see someone had sewn the wound together with coarse stitches.

"I was struck there by a mine fragment," she said. "Two years ago. We were traveling in my mother's jeep on a country road that had been mined by the militia. My mother died then. My brother Carlos, too, along with my friend Martin and his girlfriend, Lara."

She stretched her hand out to me.

"Get up," she said.

I grasped her hand and pulled myself up, but I still could not stand up straight. Hunched over I looked up at her.

She returned my gaze.

"I don't believe we will not meet again," I said. "I think rather that fate has brought us together and that we will never part."

"You only imagine things, Santiago. You will stay here in the tunnels, and you will be a king; and I will go with Celia, the woman with the baby, to America. Fate has nothing to do with it."

Disappointment crippled me.

"Celia has already tried to get across the border twice. The first time she was pregnant with Azul. The Migra arrested her just on the other side and sent her back. The second time was right after Azul's birth. The Migra caught her at a roadblock almost a hundred miles north of the border, and they sent her back again. It is the third time. Mario, her boyfriend and

Azul's father, is in Ohio, working as a waiter in a Mexican restaurant. She wants to go to him, and I'm going to help her get through this time."

"How are you going to help her? You don't know anything about it."

"I will stay with her to support her," she said. "On the way here, she broke her ankle."

"Then… then she needs a doctor."

She gave no answer.

"And what will become of us, Lucia? What I tell you that without you…" I broke off because the words didn't want to cross my lips.

She looked at me and smiled. "You will forget me quickly, Santiago. Quicker than you think."

She turned away and went around the wall and left. I tried to run after her, but, with the first step, I almost collapsed from the pain.

"Lucia!" I yelled after her. "Lucia! Wait!"

She heard me. I knew she heard me, but she did not stop. She went straight to the building where Bernardo was waiting. He opened the door for her, and she went inside, and Bernardo closed the door behind her.

*

Bernardo's tunnel was the one I had come through the first time I crossed to America. It began some five hundred meters away from the Red Cross Station and about three hundred meters from the Hotel Camino Real. It went approximately one hundred eighty paces directly across, under the border, and ended another hundred twenty paces farther at an old bridge over the Nogales Canal, not far from an empty brick building that had once been a large warehouse.

We waited at the beginning of the tunnel, Nila, Sombra and I.

Sombra grasped my hand. It was one a.m. The wind had strengthened; the night filled with the rumblings of thunder. Almost without interruption, lightning flashed around us; sometimes three or four strikes at the same time. Their stark light hit Nila's face. She crouched opposite me on the canal bank, her back turned to the wind.

"I can't stay any longer," she shouted to me. "Flaco wants me to be with him when the drug people come through the tunnel."

"They probably went through long ago," said Sombra. "As soon as it begins to rain, nobody else will be coming through."

"Could well be." In the flash of a lightning striking not far from us, Nila looked up at the sky.

"Jesus Maria, now..." Nila's words were drowned out by the crash which burst seconds later causing the earth to shake as if it was ripped open wide. The street lamps we could see looking out from the tunnel entrance flickered, went out, lit once again and then went out again. I ran up to the street. The lights had gone out in the entire city. Only over there, on the other side of the border, in Nogales, Arizona, they were still on. Like a promise. As if it were a fantasyland where the lights never go out.

A police siren howled. The headlights of a car parked at the Hotel Camino Real turned on. Ghost-like shadows moved along a wall of torn election posters.

"I'm going now," Nila shouted to me.

"Good luck."

She ran across the street and through the light from parked cars. Lightning flashed in the darkness. It began to rain, and Sombra ducked as if she could protect herself from it. A drumroll of ice-cold raindrops beat down on us from one second to the next.

"They have to go through now!" Sombra shouted to me. "In fifteen minutes, it'll be too late!"

I reached for a clear plastic bag the wind had blown across the street and hurried to wrap the revolver with it. I looked up to the Red Cross Station, where all the lights had also gone out. With the next lightning flash, I saw silhouettes of people coming out of the small building where I had met Lucia.

"They're coming!" Sombra pointed into the dark. "There they are!"

Flashlights turned on. In their beams, the rain looked like shiny metal rods. The wind whipped the rain into our faces. We had to duck to withstand its force. Sombra held tightly onto my arm. Water was already flowing in the canal and building up at the tunnel's entrance. The canal began to fill. It was a few moments before the water reached its highest level and rushed into the tunnel. The flashlights danced toward us in the rain.

"Hurry up!" I yelled. "Come on! C'mon!" I shined a flashlight on their path. The light was weak, but they must have seen it. I heard Lucia call my name.

"Santiago."

"Over here. Come on. Hurry up."

They came toward us, led by two polleros whose lights Sombra and I had seen. Crowded together in the canal, they ran toward the tunnel, silhouettes of men, women, and children who followed the polleros, trusting them to guide them safely to a promised land.

At the end of the tunnel, I laid the board against the lower edge of the tunnel so climbing into it would be easier. The backed-up water was already half a meter high. The polleros helped the first people up.

"Women and little children first!" they shouted.

A few men pushed forward, climbed to the tunnel and pulled

the children up as they were held up to them. The children cried. The men roared and cursed and pulled up the mothers. "Run through the tunnel," they shouted at the women and children. "Run! Run as fast as you can!"

"One of you first," a man said to the polleros now standing waist deep in the water. One of them was a kid. "You know the way, and you have flashlights."

One of the polleros climbed in. "Follow me!" he shouted, and he illuminated the tunnel. "Quickly! Quickly! Hold on to one another!"

They followed him and his beam of light into the black hole where the water swept away garbage from a previous flood.

"Do you see your girl?" Sombra yelled.

"There!" I pointed to the two stragglers in the canal who were about thirty paces from the tunnel.

Lucia was dragging Celia and her baby forward. They waded into knee-deep water that was getting deeper the closer they got to the entrance. Celia's face was bloody. She seemed to scream, but I didn't hear her voice through the deafening thunder. Sombra and I ran to them to help, but as I tried to grasp Celia's arm, she evaded me.

Lucia screamed at her, telling her I was her friend Santiago, the one she had talked about.

"Where is your cat?" I shouted to her.

"Gone!"

"Gone?"

"The water scared her!" She shrugged her shoulders helplessly. "She is terrified of water!"

"Tell Celia she should give the baby to Sombra!" I yelled.

Celia did not want to. She pressed the baby to herself under her wet blanket. Meanwhile, the water had climbed so high it gushed into the tunnel. It was up to the armpits of the pollero who held the board in place until the last of the group disappeared into the tunnel. Then the young one turned to us.

"Hurry up!" he yelled in a pitched voice. "Don't waste any more time!"

I glanced back and noticed more people climbing down the embankment into the canal. I grabbed Celia by the arm and pulled her along as fast as I could. I saw Sombra and Lucia take each other by the hand and fight through the rushing water together, helping each other get into the tunnel. The kid lost his grip on the board as he stretched his hand out to us. We shoved Celia up, but she slipped out of the pollero's grasp and fell back over me into the water. The other pollero caught her by her dress, and we pulled her to the edge of the tunnel and heaved her up.

"Go run, Celia!" Lucia screamed.

The pollero in the tunnel wanted Celia to go to him, but she was afraid because the group had already spread out too far.

"Go ahead!" I shouted to the pollero.

He shook his head and moved as if to jump out of the tunnel into the canal. Lightning illuminated the panic in his face.

"You go with her!" I roared at him, and I reached under my shirt and pulled the plastic-wrapped gun out of the waistband of my pants. Despite the wrapping, he recognized it as a gun. He cursed, turned around and ran into the tunnel as quickly as he could and began to shout for help. Sombra helped Lucia up, and Lucia knelt at the edge of the tunnel and pulled up Sombra. The pollero in the tunnel came back with two more men and a woman. The woman supported Celia. One of the men grabbed Sombra by the arm. The kid tried to pull Lucia with him, but she tugged herself loose. "Just go!" she yelled at him. "Go! I'll come after you!" The kid turned and followed the pollero with the flashlight. I still stood in the canal, trying to hold the gun above water and waiting for the last of the polleros to climb into the tunnel, but he stopped and shone his light on me.

"Come on, I'll help you!"

He shook his head. "You go first!"

He reached for the edge of the tunnel with his free hand, pulled me out of the water and heaved me up. When I got up and turned toward the pollero, I saw him on all fours, climbing the embankment of the canal. He ran for his life; running back to security. I could have shot him, but I didn't even raise the revolver. I did not see him fleeing along the canal, which had turned into a roaring stream. I turned and followed the people and the dancing beams of light in front of me.

*

The pollero in the lead screamed for help, shouting the name of a man leading another group.

Our little group consisted of the pollero, Celia and her baby, Azul, an older man with a beard named Vicente and a younger man, Ramon, who held Sombra by the hand. Lucia and an older woman named Anna supported Celia. I brought up the rear with the plastic-wrapped gun still in my hand.

I began to count my steps as I had the first time. Progress was difficult; the tunnel was full of floating stuff blocking the way. Also, the water level was climbing by the second. It already was above my knees before we had gone twenty steps into the tunnel.

The thunder echoed through the tunnel and mixed with the rushing water. The man in front of me got hung up on a piece of bent iron looming out of some uprooted brush. He tried to free himself by kicking at the piece of metal with his other foot. The kicking caused him to lose his balance and fall. I wanted to grab him by his poncho, but just then, a wave struck us from behind sweeping my legs out from under me. As I got back onto my feet, the water sloshed over me. I heard someone scream.

It was the pollero's voice. A hard object bumped into my legs. I fell in and with one hand I found something to grab and hold on to. With the other one, I was still clutching the revolver. A beam of light fell on me.

"Come on!" the pollero screamed. "Hurry!"

We hurried on. The man who had been in front of me was now behind me. I caught up with Sombra and the woman. Sombra held a flashlight we had found in the Subaru. She pointed it at me as she stumbled on, pushed by the water. Everything started to happen so quickly, that I didn't think of counting my steps. Meanwhile, the water was now up to my hips.

The pollero reached the drainage shaft which led upward. It was the one I had used to climb out of the tunnel the first time. Panicking, he grabbed the first rung and pulled himself up to get out of the water. He climbed a few rungs as quickly as he could. In the light of his flashlight, I saw Anna reaching for the first rung, but she first grasped nothing. Then one of the pollero's legs appeared and she grabbed it. From above, the man yelled at her to let go. Anna clamped herself to him with both hands. Then, in the light beam, the pollero's other leg appeared. Angrily, he kicked at Anna's head and face. With a cry, she let go of the leg and fell backward into the raging water shooting down the tunnel, carrying her along.

Lucia turned to me. She was directly below the drainage shaft the pollero had climbed.

"Give me your revolver," she cried with a wild look in her eyes.

Whenever possible, I had kept my hand with the gun above the water; it was my only possession that meant anything to me.

"Your revolver!" Lucia screamed.

I forced myself past Ramon and found myself at the shaft. Above me, I saw the pollero hanging on the rungs, ready to kick anyone who came near him. Blue light fell through the openings of the drain cover. Rainwater ran down the walls as if someone above was pouring buckets full into the gutter.

I pointed the revolver at him.

"Come down and help us," I yelled.

"Help yourselves," he shouted back.

He climbed higher until he banged his head on the drain cover, the one I had once pushed up. He tried to push it up with his shoulder, but the cover did not yield this time.

Meanwhile, Lucia had taken the baby from Celia and given it to Sombra. With both arms, she heaved Celia up until she could grab hold of the rungs.

"Climb," Lucia said to her when Celia looked around for the baby. "Climb to him. Sombra will bring your child."

Celia obeyed. Up above, the pollero was still working on the drain cover. As Celia came up to him, he screamed that the exit was barred. Water poured in swells through the lid over him and Celia. Below, in the tunnel, we were scarcely able to fight against the raging of the water. We stood close, held each other and tried to keep our heads above water.

Lucia took the baby, and Ramon helped Sombra up to the rungs. She immediately reached down for the baby with her right arm. Lucia gave it to her, and Sombra climbed higher up.

"You're next," said Ramon, after Sombra and the baby were secure. He wanted to help Lucia up into the shaft, but she shook her head. "You go first."

Ramon, who was perhaps twenty years old, grabbed the first rung, pulled himself up and grabbed the second rung with his other hand.

Lucia turned to the older man. "Let's go! You're next!"

The older man was having trouble keeping himself above water.

"There's not enough room here for everybody," the pollero shouted from above.

"Then make yourself smaller!" Ramon yelled back at him. "Make yourself smaller!"

"Still, there's not enough room for everyone!"

The pollero made himself small, and Celia climbed a rung higher.

Vicente, the man with the beard, still did not want to go up the shaft ahead of Lucia.

"You go first," he demanded of her. "Then you can help me up."

A wave, loaded with tangled debris, hit me, and I nearly lost my footing. With one hand, I grasped the lowest rung and pulled myself out of the water, which was pulling at me with unrelenting strength. I wasn't able to grasp the next rung, because I was still holding the revolver in my other hand.

"Throw it away," cried Sombra from above. "Throw away the gun, Santiago."

I didn't consider following her order. But I sensed I would not be able to hold on much longer. My arm seemed about to separate from my body, as if sinews and muscles would tear apart. I screamed the pain into the wild rush of the water, clenching my teeth. I would have had to let go in the next second, but Izan, a strong young man who traveled alone like me, grabbed both my legs with his arms and tried to heave me up. The current and my weight caused him to lose his balance. He disappeared under the water, his hand grasping at nothing. I saw his head reappear, and I saw the fear in his wide eyes and the pale blue light on his gleaming face. Then he was gone.

Lucia, who was still reaching for Izan, was now directly under me, and she grabbed one of my legs and held onto me in desperation. The current tried to tear her away, down into the floodwater rushing to America. Helpless myself, I watched her fight with the last of her strength, but she couldn't manage to pull herself up to me. I let go of the rung to help her and fell over her, back into the water. Underwater my back hit against something unwieldy, upon which I resisted the current with all my strength. When I came up again, Lucia was being swirled around so close to me she struck my shoulder hard with her elbow. She clamped herself onto me, and I finally let go of the gun so both hands were free. I grabbed her by the arm, and with my other hand, I grasped for the lowest rung. Ramon reached down and caught me by the wrist. I tried to pull myself up with his help, and, for a moment, it seemed as if I would be able to do it, but then I felt Lucia begin to slip out of my grip. I let go of the rung to grab her with my other hand, but Ramon held me with both hands while Sombra held onto him. "Let go!" I screamed.

Beneath me, Lucia was swept away. For a moment, I saw her come up to the light. I saw her arms beating about, saw her head, her hair. I saw how she was pushed and swirled around and how one of her legs appeared out of the flood and struck the wet concrete wall. I saw her head once more, a shadow suddenly disappearing into the darkness of the tunnel. Then I didn't see her anymore.

"Hold onto the rung!" yelled Ramon. "Hold on tight, man!"

I didn't want to. I wanted to jump in, but Sombra's voice held me back.

"Santiago!" she shouted. "Santiago, she will be waiting for us at the end of the tunnel!"

At the end of the tunnel? How far was that? Two hundred steps? No, fewer. I grasped for the rung with my other hand. Water struck me in the face when I looked up. The pollero pointed the flashlight down at me. With a last effort, I pulled myself up. I made myself as small as I could. Under me, on the two lowest rungs, one more could have had a place, but nobody else came. I stared into the foaming stream shooting by scarcely a meter beneath me, expecting Lucia to appear. There, an arm. For a few seconds, it appeared out of the water, only to disappear the next moment. The arm was not an arm. The arm was a branch shooting out of the water, turning in the flashlight beam and then disappearing into the tunnel.

"Lucia!"

My voice was drowned out by the rush of the flood.

*

We crouched on the rungs in the drain shaft. At the bottom, it was about two meters wide, and it became narrower at the top. The pollero tried to push up the drain cover several times, but he didn't succeed. He was a small, lightly built man, but he shielded us against the water pouring in from above with his thin, crumpled body while he was struck fully by it.

The storm raged. Thunder clapped through the drain cover. The lightning's illumination went over us on its way into the depths. I heard Celia and Ramon praying. Sombra asked the pollero if there was room enough for her on the upper rungs so they both, with their combined strength, could heave the drain cover from the opening. The pollero answered that there wasn't even enough space for him up there.

"We have to cry for help!" Sombra said.

Celia began to scream. She had the baby pressed to herself, and she screamed simply out of despair.

The pollero kicked at her.

"Be quiet, woman! If the Migra discovers us, we're done!"

More and more, the water flowed through the slots in the drain cover while less and less air got in. The air we were breathing was warm and humid and used up.

"How is the baby?" I heard Sombra ask.

Celia took the baby out from under her wrap. It didn't move, and its eyes were closed. The pollero shined his flashlight on its face.

"My baby!" Celia cried out. "Maybe it's dead!"

"Then let it fall," said the pollero. "A dead baby will only hinder you. Besides, it needs—"

"The baby didn't die," Sombra interrupted. "It just moved an arm."

Celia put the baby back in her wrap. The pollero rammed his shoulder against the underside of the drain cover, but the heavy iron grating didn't give way a millimeter.

"Help me, Jesus and Mary!" the pollero begged and beat against the cover with his bent arm to loosen it. "I will never ask you for anything again; this I promise you. Even when I'm on my deathbed, I will not whine for your blessing as my father did when the Devil took his soul. I am an honorable person. A guide for the lost and desperate to cross the border, but nevertheless—"

"Why should Jesus and Mary listen to your babbling?" Ramon yelled. "Maybe it would be better if you shouted for help so the Migra could take us out of this hole."

"No, not the Migra," cried Celia. "Our long journey would have been in vain."

"So, we have to hold out," said Ramon. "When it stops raining, there will also be less water."

We held out. For almost two hours. The air was so bad, we barely got enough oxygen. The storm had let up, and less water was coming from above us. But the slots in the drain cover were plugged with trash. The pollero tried to free up the openings by pulling the wet and filthy stuff through. Plastic and paper. A bag from McDonald's. The insole of a shoe. A baseball cap the pollero put on his head because he had lost his.

Coolness seeped into the tunnel with the fresh air from above. We heard police sirens. The American ones sounded different than those in Mexico. The pollero tried again to move the drain cover. In vain. He cursed God and the world and us; we had forced him to go into the tunnel.

"You were well paid for it," Sombra interrupted his cursing. "Instead of yammering and complaining, call for help so somebody will come and raise the jammed lid."

It began to rain again.

"Que mierda, the Migra will find us," cursed the pollero.

"It doesn't make any difference to me who finds us!" shouted Sombra. "We can't wait here until there's no more water in the tunnel. With this storm, that could be days from now."

"I don't want to go back," sobbed Celia. "I don't want to go back again!"

"Think of your baby, Celia," warned Sombra. "It is wet and cold. If nobody finds us, your baby will die."

Under her soaked wrap, Celia pressed the baby tighter to herself.

"Let's get out of here!" said Ramon. He began to yell for help and, after a while, we all joined in. But nobody came to help us. Our voices echoed unheard on the empty lot where the cold rain beat down.

The rain let up and finally stopped. The pollero pointed his flashlight down the shaft at the foaming water flowing by just under the bottom rung.

"It's going down," the man shouted from above. "Thank God. Mary, Mother of God, let me kiss your feet." Then he pointed the flashlight to my face. "Do you see, my friend? The water level is going down."

I let myself down and slid my feet into the cold water until I felt the bottom of the tunnel. The water reached up to my chin, but the current had become weaker. I felt around under the surface of the foaming water for the thing I had gotten a grip on earlier. It was no longer there, but I felt around and found something soft to grab.

I grabbed with my other hand and braced myself backward against the current. Whatever I had grabbed was moveable. I pulled at it with all my strength, and suddenly, there appeared the head of a person, a shoulder, and a naked arm. I could see that it was not Lucia I had pulled out of the water. It was a man who was bald and had a mustache. I held him by a torn shirt that was wound around his neck. At first, I wanted to let go of him, but then I pulled him to me against the current and turned him so they could look at his face.

"Any of you know him?"

"That is Adriano Pinto," said Celia so softly that I could scarcely hear her.

"Adriano Pinto," Ramon confirmed. "What happened to him? Did he drown?"

"He is dead," I said. "Either drowned or he got strangled by his shirt." I let go of him, and the current carried him away.

"Look, the water's going down!" shouted Sombra. "It's going down slowly."

Ramon climbed down and dropped into the water. We joined hands, and I felt for obstacles with my other hand. After a few meters, Señor Pinto appeared once again in front of us. He was hanging from a branch. Now his eyes were open, and he stared at me with reproach, as if I had brought about his death. I let go of Ramon's hand, freed the body of Señor Pinto from the branch and gave him a push away from me.

Sombra shouted,

"Santiago, please don't leave us behind."

I was so distraught I actually would have gone to the end of the tunnel without any thought for the others.

"We've got to help them!" Ramon said.

We turned around and worked our way against the current, back to where Celia, Sombra, and the pollero were hanging tightly to the iron rungs.

"We can go farther down the tunnel," Ramon shouted to them. "We've got to try to get out of here!"

One after another, they climbed down; last was the pollero with the flashlight. Scared because the water was up to his neck, he started to climb back. I grabbed him by the arm. "Give me the flashlight! Then you can do whatever you want!"

"Why should I give you my flashlight? You—"

"Because I'm telling you," I cut him off.

"Give Santiago the light!" Sombra told him coldly. She was standing behind him with an arm around Celia.

The pollero probably remembered that she was a friend of Bernardo's, and he gave me the flashlight.

*

The water diminished. When we reached the group ahead of us, the water reached only to my chest. Even the kids who had made it that far, had no more trouble keeping their head above water. We stopped at the next drainage shaft and looked up. The rain had nearly stopped. We heard the sirens and motors of patrol cars.

I turned the flashlight over to Sombra, and I climbed to the drain cover and shoved against it with all the strength I could muster, but it wouldn't move.

I climbed back down into the tunnel. Sombra gave me the flashlight and, just as I was about to proceed, I heard a cough that seemed to come from in the tunnel in front of us. I tried to rush on, lost my footing and dove forward into the water, but there was no one there for me to grab. Disappointed, I stopped, but the current threw me around, I swallowed a lot of water before I came back up. I had never been a good swimmer. I had been afraid of water for as long as I could remember. Fear of the animals living in water. Snakes. Electric eels. Fish with poisonous spines.

As I turned around, my foot struck something hard lying on the bottom. I bent over and probed it with my hand. The water ran in my ear. I started to stand up when my finger encountered a piece of iron. I grabbed it and pulled it out of the water. It was a heavy pipe wrench. I took it by the handle and went back to the others. Once again, I climbed the shaft.

I used the pipe wrench as a hammer, and I struck the iron frame of the drain cover several times with all my strength. Then I pushed once more against it with my shoulder and the cover gave way. I gave out a cry of triumph as it tipped from my shoulder and I was able to shove it from the shaft opening with my hand.

Down below, in the tunnel, Sombra, Celia, Ramon and the pollero cheered as if I had knocked down the door to Paradise for them. Celia gave her baby to Sombra. Ramon and the pollero heaved her up out of the water so she could grasp the bottom step. But Celia was so exhausted she no longer had the strength to get to the next rung. I climbed down and gave her my hand and all of us managed to climb to the opening. I crawled out, looked around quickly and then helped Celia out. Next was Sombra. She brought the baby up with her. Behind her came Ramon. The pollero stayed below.

"I'm going back," he shouted to us. "I haven't lost anything in America. Good luck to you all. Don't let the Migra catch you."

He disappeared into the tunnel.

"Good luck," Sombra called to him.

"Let us all go back," sobbed Celia. She looked fearfully in every direction. But the streets were empty. Wet and empty. It was no longer raining. The night air was clear, and a cold wind blew through the city. In the distance, thunder rumbled and, once in a while, lightning reflected off the clouds.

An American ambulance raced by us, its siren screaming and lights flashing.

"We've made it, and now I'll never go back," said Ramon. "First, we have to find someplace dry where we can hide." He looked at me questioningly, then at Sombra. Sombra said, not far from her parents' house at the outskirts of the city, there was a motel that could take them in.

"I'm going to the end of the tunnel," I said. "I have to find Lucia. "

"Call me in the morning," Sombra yelled after me as I ran down the street.

*

Where the tunnel emptied into the Nogales Canal, the streets were blocked by more than a dozen cars and trucks from the police and the border patrol, some fire trucks and several ambulances. Searchlights illuminated the tunnel exit and the canal for a distance of more than a hundred meters. A brown foaming bilge swirled between the steep embankments against a gigantic bulldozer scooping up dripping loads of trash and rubble to be dumped on top of the embankment.

Firefighters in their bright yellow overalls with long pickaxes were poking around in the water. They pulled out all sorts of stuff the flood had carried along: debris from houses that had lost their hold on weakened slopes and slid downhill with the soil, mattresses, clothing, drowned house pets and the swollen carcass of a dairy cow. They also recovered a piece of an inflatable rowboat and a large package of marijuana, wrapped in plastic. And next to the ambulances, the bodies of drowned people lay on the asphalt of a blocked-off street. Alternating red and blue light outlined the forms of human bodies.

I approached this place dazed and exhausted from running. My only thought was with Lucia, and it almost drove me crazy. People lined up along yellow police tape so they could watch the rescue. Through all the other noise I heard the bulldozer and the voices coming out of the two-way radios. I heard Nila's voice calling my name. But, without paying attention to all this, I forced myself through the people, shoving aside anyone who tried to stop me. A police officer grabbed my shirt as I slipped right under the blockade.

"Get the hell back, kid!"

I pointed at the body on the edge of the canal. "Mi hermana!" I yelled to him.

The police officer turned to the people crowded close on the edge of the street. Men with naked white torsos and bare feet, clothed only in pajama pants, and women who had thrown on house coats.

"What the hell did he say?" the police officer shouted at them.

"Mi hermana!" I said and tried to tear myself loose, but his grip was that of a man who was trained to grab people.

"His sister!" one of the women yelled. "He believes his sister is among those dead people there."

"His sister?"

"Hermana, that's 'sister' in Spanish."

The police officer spoke into a walkie-talkie. Another police officer turned toward us. He was one of the two I had seen in the patrol car when I was walking with Sombra.

"Is there a woman among those stiffs there, Joe?"

"A woman?"

"He's looking for his sister."

"There are two women." The officer came over. "Don't I know you, kid? Didn't I see you with Sombra?"

I understood nothing of what he said.

"He's asking you if he's seen you with a girl named Sombra," someone explained.

"Yes," I answered. "Sombra's a friend of mine."

"You believe your sister is lying there?" the officer asked me in broken Spanish.

"Yes! I lost my sister."

"I'll take him, Jack," the police officer said. He grabbed me by the arm as the other policeman let go.

"Come on," he said, and he led me across the street where an officer of the Migra was standing with other police. A large dog bared his teeth and growled like he wanted to swallow me. The Migra officer, an American of Mexican descent who was holding the dog on a leash, turned toward us.

"Who the fuck is he?" he asked the policeman.

"He's okay, Tony. He's looking for his sister."

As we approached the corpses, the policeman asked my name in Spanish.

"Santiago Molina," I said

"And your sister's?"

"Lucia."

A young woman wearing a raincoat and rubber gloves climbed out of the ambulance and approached us.

"He thinks his sister is one of them," the policeman said to her. The young woman looked at me.

"I hope not," she said. "Well, you people never learn, do you? This border is a treacherous piece of this world. Too many people have died, just trying to cross it."

"His name is Santiago," said the policeman. "His sister's name is Lucia."

The young woman raised the cover on the first corpse a little. Under it lay a woman I had never seen before.

"Is that her?" the policeman asked me.

I shook my head.

"Thank God," said the woman as she pointed at the next corpse. "That's not your sister, kid. That's a man."

"Can I see him?"

She looked at me. "Were you with them in the tunnel when—" She broke off when she saw my dirtied and torn pants and the scrapes on my arms and hands. She turned to the policeman. "Joe, do you think what I think?"

"Never mind, Mary. The kid is looking for some people."

She raised the covering from the corpse of the man. My stomach turned. There lay Señor Pinto, whose body I had already seen in the tunnel.

"You know him?" the young woman asked me.

"Do you know him?" the policeman asked in Spanish.

I shook my head.

"Thank God," said the woman.

She raised the cloth from the next corpse. An older woman with gray hair lay there in the wet dirt, her eyes wide open. The young woman bent over her and tried to close her eyelids with a touch of her hand. It didn't work.

"So far, these are the only ones we recovered," the police officer said. "Somebody you know?"

"No."

The next corpse was that of a young boy. He had a gaping wound on his forehead and his arms were completely twisted away from his body.

The police officer and the woman looked at me.

"No," I said.

On the bank of the canal, some twenty paces away, one of the firefighters shouted that he had a dead body on his hook. Although it was hard for me to understand his agitated words, I knew what he meant. The young woman ran along the embankment where a few firefighters formed a chain in the rapidly flowing water. The man at the end went under up to his head and came up with a body. Together, they pulled it out of the water, out of the jumble of branches and trash. They dragged it up the embankment and I recognized him when his head turned to one side, and one of the spotlights shone directly in his face. It was Izan.

"This one you know," said the police officer, who had let go of my arm.

"His name is Izan," I said.

We went to where Izan lay on the ground. Someone brought a machine, a defrilibrator, and a man smeared clear gel on Izan and another man pressed two large black paddles to Izan's bare chest.

"All clear!" somebody shouted.

Izan was hit by an electric shock, and his body suddenly writhed under the man and immediately fell back limply.

"All clear!" shouted the man. And again and again. "All clear! All clear!" Finally he gave up. "That's it. This guy's had it. No way, he's coming back."

The man heaved himself up and looked around as if he were looking for someone.

"This kid knows the man," said the police officer next to me.

"Can you identify him for us?" the man who had tried to bring Izan back to life asked me, first in English and then in Spanish. "Just a name, maybe. It would help us to contact his family."

"His name is Izan," I said. "I don't know anything more about him."

"The kid here is looking for his sister," explained the police officer. The man had already turned around. He went back to one of the ambulances.

"Maybe your sister managed to get through," said the police officer to me in Spanish to raise my hopes. "Many got through before we got here and are long gone. The Migra snapped up some of them farther down the canal trying to hide in a shack."

We were standing on the embankment, and I looked into the canal, but the water was so dirty not even the searchlights could penetrate it.

"Let's go, kid," said the police officer. "I can't let you stay here."

He took me by the arm. I thought about pulling loose and running away, but I no longer had the strength. We turned away from the canal and were about to cross the street when the noise of the bulldozer suddenly stopped. A man's voice shouted something. The police officer looked around, and I heard him say, "God damn, they got another one." I turned back and even before I saw what the bulldozer had in its bucket, I knew Lucia had not made it.

I tore myself loose and ran back along the embankment. Hands tried to stop me, but I struck them aside or I ducked under them. I slid down the embankment and into the water and out to the bulldozer. I jumped up onto it, and I swung onto its extended arm where the bucket hung. With one hand, I got a hold on the edge of the bucket. I pulled myself up, swung a leg over the edge and dropped into the bucket. And there she lay, in the midst of all the mud and garbage. One arm buried under her body, with the other arm stretched out as if she was trying to protect herself from something, from one of the thorn-covered branches sticking out of the dirt, or from the bent car bumper laying crossways over the bucket. I pulled the stuff away from her, grabbed her and raised her lifeless body up to where I could take her in my arms. There I knelt with her. I knelt in the mud in the bucket and cried my heart out of my body until I had no more voice.

*

The next day, they took me out of the barred cell at the Migra, where I had spent the night with two dozen other illegal immigrants.

Sombra and her parents stood outside in the sun. Tears came to Sombra's eyes as we looked at each other. We embraced and her mother hugged us both, while her father, wearing his uniform with the badge of the Migra, acted as if he were unconcerned.

I was dazed. I hadn't slept. I sought answers. I cursed the one people had so often told me was the "Almighty". Holding all the strings in His hand, he watches over his children as a loving father." I had wished for nothing more and nothing less for Lucia. Only that she would come through. That she would have succeeded on behalf of all the others who hadn't received a chance. It had nothing to do with her and me, had nothing to do with love.

I had known the day before, when we saw each other again, that things had become different. Now, it seemed as if an eternity had passed since we had met for the first time on a desert country road, tired of dreaming alone, tired of going my way alone so far away from home. The day I met Lucia I was still a boy, but it was also the day I became a man.

Now I could feel nothing of what I once felt. No hate, no love, no rage. Nothing. Who I once was had died.

Sombra took me by the hand. She had tears in her eyes.

Her father said to me, "They want you to look at all of them again, to identify the ones you recognize."

We went to the morgue. Police officers and officers of the Migra went with us. They showed me the dead, and they were nothing but corpses. I recognized Izan again. And Anna. Nobody else.

Then I stood before Lucia. She lay there, clean and still. She was white as snow, though not a white person. I saw the scar on her leg, a reminder from her fighting against the powerful. Her face, in which everything fit together, even now it had been stitched together, this wonderfully beautiful face I had never kissed. I stepped closer to her. Someone wanted to hold me back, but a soft voice said it was okay for me to stay. Lucia's eyes were closed. I would have liked to have seen her eyes once again. One more time. I placed a hand on her arm and bent over her and kissed her lips, and my tears fell on her face. Carefully I wiped my tears from her skin with my fingers, and I prayed for the first time in a long, long while. I prayed someone would one day lead me to where she was now.

As I turned from Lucia, my hand sought Sombra's, and we held hands as we went out into the sunlight.

*

On that same day, they brought me, and all the others, back across the border and delivered us to the cops of Grupo Beta.

There were people out everywhere, cleaning up the city, removing signs left over from the storm.

We were locked in a cell and set free the next day.

I went down to the tunnels and asked for Flaco. Then I went through the city looking for the cat. I didn't find the cat, but I found Flaco in Manny's Bar.

"Where were you all this time?" he asked me as if nothing had happened.

"On the other side," I said in my native language, which he did not understand. He looked at me, bewildered and exchanged a quick glance with Manny.

"Are you okay?"

I nodded and told him I had become a different person, and I was no longer the person he knew. I also said it in my language, in the tongue of the Tzotzil.

Behind the bar, Manny quickly crossed himself. He seemed to be afraid of me.

"Man, are those the voices you heard? The voices of your ancestors?" asked Flaco.

I did not answer.

"I always knew there was something wrong with your head," said Flaco. "Bring him a Coke, Manny." Flaco put his arm across my shoulders and pulled me closer. "You did well, my friend," he whispered to me.

I didn't say anything. Manny brought me a Coke.

"Shot in the neck," he said. "The cops found him in the park this morning, not a hundred meters from the place where Tomo got killed."

Now I started to realize he was talking about Bernardo, and he believed I was the one who wasted him.

"Why are you not saying anything, my friend?" he asked.

"Because I feel like being dead," I said.

Manny heard it. "Jesus, Maria," he said. "Go home, kid."

I slid off the barstool and left. I didn't want to go home. I had a new life and a new dream. So, I went through the city and the tunnel back to America. I went through Nogales, Arizona. I walked by McDonald's and T.T.'s Saloon, and I walked down a steep, potholed street and up to the school. I went to the carwash and through the alleys and by old, empty brick buildings and across the railroad tracks and along the river flowing north. I saw the parked patrol car with the two police officers, and they looked across and waved to me, and I went out of the city into open land, through high yellow grass and onto an unpaved road where the red clay clung to my shoes. Somewhere, I sat in the shade of a cottonwood tree.

As it became night, I went back into the city and crept to where I had already crept a few times. I made myself small in that wrecked car and waited for morning and for Sombra. I waited for a new beginning.

**

ACTEAL, Mexico

"Yesterday, a group of armed men raided an Indian village. They opened fire with automatic weapons, and they also shot down those who were fleeing, including women with their children. In total, 45 people were killed in this worst incident since the rebellion of three years earlier."

The Arizona Daily Star, December 24, 1997

"Mexico's Zapatista rebel leader broke off all contacts with the government yesterday and called upon supporters to protest against an Indian-rights bill he said fails to meet rebel demands.

The Zapatistas want regional autonomy on issues like native languages and traditional government and law based on councils of elders or village assemblies."

The Seattle Times, April 30, 2001

CONTENTS

Books in German by ARAVAIPA:

Werner J. Egli:

Tunnel Kids	978-3-03864-010-3
Heul doch den Mond an	978-3-03864-008-0
Der erste Schuss	978-3-03864-004-2
Der letzte Kampf des Tigers	978-3-03864-000-4
Black Shark	978-3-03864-002-8
Aus den Augen, voll im Sinn	978-3-03864-003-5

Hubert Flattinger:

Baboon	978-3-03864-001-1
Sommersprossen auf dem Asphalt	978-3-03864-006-6

Werner Färber:

Willst du Stress	978-3-03864-005-9

Aravaipa Publishing: www.aravaipa.ch